This issue is a revival, a call to the sweet sweat of the summer celebration. This is the breath of wind that sweeps before the storm, that tells us of things to come and of things that will disappear when we look away. These stories are the seeds and fruits that have lain dormant for some time, and now they are all sprouting.

Here are stories about revenge, stories about justice, stories about what we get when we ask for too much without understanding the triumverate of suggestion, desperation, and denial. And there are stories of loss and sorrow and hope, because the wheel always turns. What was returns, and what is expires. On and on, above and below.

This is a new season of Underland Arcana.

Underland Arcana is published on a seasonal basis. This issue is published in conjunction with the summer solstice, when air and water mix to become steam and sweat.

EDITOR
Mark Teppo

SIGIL ART
Andrew Penn Romine

PUBLISHER
Underland Press
Clackamas, OR, USA

At noon, there is no shadow without presence . . .

UNDERLAND ARCANA

~ 12 ~

Underland Press

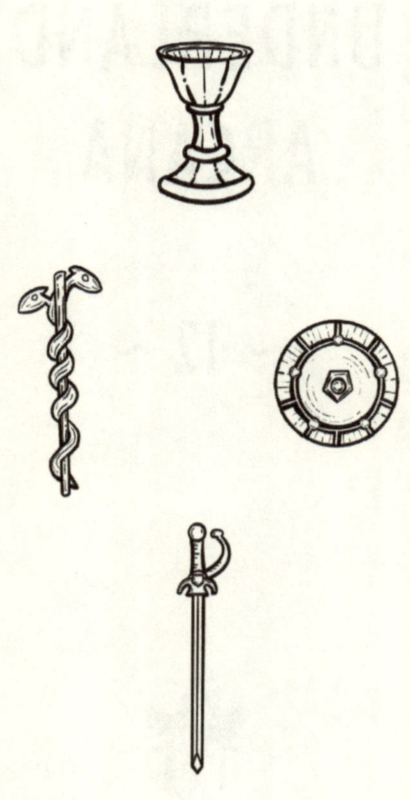

Contents

vii ~ ~ ~ *Editorial: The Wheel Turns Round*

1 ~ ~ ~ *A Pilgrimage* ~ Daniel David Froid

21 ~ ~ ~ *The Breath Before the Cut* ~ Megan Lee Beals

29 ~ ~ ~ *Lepid Little Lies* ~ Pen Anderson

59 ~ ~ ~ *For Sale: A House in Snatches* ~ Elou Carroll

71 ~ ~ ~ *Bring Me the Head of Louise Michel!* ~ Basile Lebret

97 ~ ~ ~ *Séance at the Jukebox* ~ Brian U. Garrison

99 ~ ~ ~ *Jesus Christ & Snow White* ~ H. L. Fullerton

123 ~ ~ ~ *Be Careful What You Wish For* ~ Jetse de Vries

141 ~ ~ ~ *Wolf's Clothing* ~ Jonathan Wood

159 ~ ~ ~ *In Time With the Ocean* ~ Devan Barlow

171 ~ ~ ~ *The Alphabet of Dread* ~ Ben Curl

183 ~ ~ ~ *Contributor Bios*

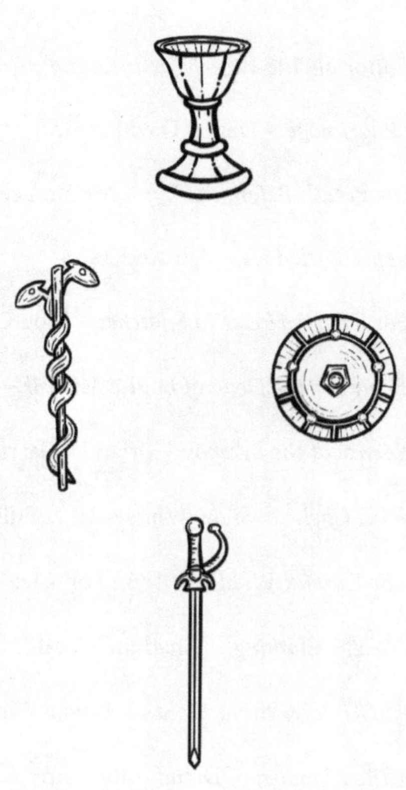

The Wheel Turns Round

I am weary of dystopian visions, and I know I am not alone in this weariness. Filmmakers used to have to spend an inordinate amount of time and/or money to create a satisfying dystopian landscape. These days? Well, they don't have to drive far to find a decaying factory or a blasted landscape filled with dust and the rotting stumps of an abandoned civilization. Just past the edge of town, you hear? Under the overpass for the interchange that was never finished—government ran out of money, you see, or maybe those in power found us too contrary and they hoped we'd wander off.

This used to be the make-believe of science fiction. Now, it's—well, it's not so make-believe any more. Our weariness stems from just getting up in the morning. It's in our coffee. It's reflected in the eyes of our pets and friends and loved ones as they try not to stare into the distance. And those who persist in writing about it? Well, they don't celebrate it. It's not a "hip" milieu to for your fiction. Those who persist, however, they call it "cli-fi" or "hope-punk," in an effort to find something uplifting in their storytelling.

We keep trying, don't we?

As a part-time bookseller, it is fascinating to watch the turn of the seasons, as far as trends and notions and fulsome flavors go. A year or two into a new administration, thrillers adjust to reflect the current trend in national paranoia. The more this trend leans supernatural, the more confidence the public has in the administration. We stop worrying about clean water, public infrastructure, and rot at a national level. We go back to fretting about monsters and things that deny common sense.

As I write this introduction, we're deep in a fascination with butchers, billionaires, and bad boys—wounded ducks who need someone to truly love them. "He may be a monster, but he loves me, so it's all okay."

I'll leave it to you to decide what this says about where we're at right now.

The wheel turns round, as the old song goes. Things flourish, and then fall apart. Buried, they decay and transform. When the rains come again, they sprout anew. Different sprouts. Different flowers. Plant lemon seeds and up sprout oranges.

We went away for awhile. Some things changed. Some things didn't. It's the growing season again. Let's see what will sprout from the seeds we planted during the winter.

Hey now, hey now, now, sing This Corrosion to me
Hey now, hey now, now
(Like a healing hand)

May 12th, 2025

A Pilgrimage

~ Daniel David Froid

Two men decided to go on a pilgrimage. Rather, one man decided and the other agreed.

When Simon announced to Ted that he wanted to go on a pilgrimage, Ted balked, fearing that Simon had become religious. His mind summoned images of Simon in strange company, Bible-thumpers or rosary-clutchers, a long line of miserable days in which Simon shambled in anger and self-righteousness, fear and bigotry. Simon had always been a little incredulous, a little maudlin, struck by the desire to belong. Briefly, Ted wondered whether he ought to stage an intervention. All this took place as he stared at a chain of text messages.

Ted watched the dancing ellipsis appear on his screen and vanish as Simon took his time with his words and further stoked his partner's anxieties.

At last Simon's next message appeared, which took a blithe and casual tone: "Not a religious thing lol," he wrote. Ted felt chastened, though all he had so far written was a single character: "?"

Simon sent Ted a link to an article about something called "The Way of the Monk," which began with a map that showed a red line snaking across several countries in northern Europe and concluding in a small one he had never heard of called Loturia. *Was it really possible,* he thought, *that there are still countries I've never even heard of? Or is this one new?* He read on, learning about a couple of characters known only as "the monk" and "the prince"—their names apparently lost to time—who made a journey from the monk's holy grotto, "where he spent a century alone in prayer," near the castle where the sheltered and beautiful prince had grown into a sheltered and beautiful man. Their long journey took them to an isolated village. The men, who might have been lovers, had attempted to capitalize on certain talents the monk possessed for curing ailments and peering into the past and the future, and they succeeded for a time. However, the villagers' suspicion overtook their initial delight, and they convinced themselves that the strangers acted according to the devil's bidding. The men were burned at the stake, but their legend survived. Following the men's path to their fate was fast becoming—according to the article—a popular option for the curious and an alternative to a stuffy traditional pilgrimage such as, say, the Camino de Santiago.

Ted had not been aware that there was anyone alive with a taste for pilgrimages who did not also like that which could be called stuffy and traditional, but here it was. Evidently, Simon was one of them. Perhaps he was as well. After all, he liked the sound of it: a journey undertaken by two lovers, rebels, possibly sorcerers. It seemed almost romantic, even the fact of their dying, for they had only been rejected due to one community's cruelty and ignorance.

He wrote back to Simon: "This sounds cool. Never heard of this legend." Simon replied with several messages in a row affirming his own excitement. It was already a done deal, and Ted knew it. They booked their trip and began to look forward to a late-summer trip to follow the Way of the Monk.

To varying degrees, each man grew increasingly thrilled: Simon could not wait, enthralled as he was by the legend, the journey, the idea of it, the idea of their walking the path and claiming the story as theirs to share forever. As for Ted, he had tempered Simon's enthusiasm by checking where they might stay throughout the journey, categorically refusing to rough it. It was Ted who packed the right clothes and sundries, made plans to secure healthy snacks and ample water, and traced the route precisely according to the guidebook. Simon did not argue, for he wished to fulfill what had become—as he called it—his dream and, anyway, hated planning. While love would be the wrong word to describe Ted's relationship to planning, he took to it compulsively. In this way, in time, he likewise became fixated on the journey, increasingly interested in learning more about the legend and about Loturia.

And the matter of Loturia was strange. They had booked their passage to follow what was apparently a well-known route. And yet, sometimes, when he looked at a map, Ted couldn't find their destination. He blamed himself and his lack of geographical acumen, but it did seem strange. If he squinted, he thought, he could just make out the small country where they would end up—but, then again, perhaps he was wrong.

He sent away for some informative literature, which, when it arrived in the mail, cleared things up only a little. Dutifully, Ted tucked away the map they would use to follow in the footsteps of the legendary men. They would walk the same path they did and, eventually, even sail a ship that traced the same route as theirs, so long ago. And then Ted read a slim booklet, emblazoned with a logo that prominently featured an elegant drawing of a goose, which explained that Loturia was a nation-state with a rich history, one small bit of land in northern Europe, technically a peninsula, with a few stray islands alongside it. Previously very little-known, it had only recently opened up to visitors. He explained all this to Simon, who said, "Oh, so it's like the Victorians learning about Japan." "What?" Ted asked. Simon shrugged, dimly remembering something learned a decade ago.

"But how," Ted asked, "could a nation be so little-known that it doesn't even show up on maps? How is that possible?"

Simon could not answer. "It is very strange," he allowed. "I guess we'll learn more when we get there."

The guidebook also emphasized that this undertaking was a pilgrimage, not simply tourism. "It is intended that the pilgrim shed the frippery of the self's outer layers and uncover the innermost self, as the monk and the prince approached the heart of who they were—and suffered for it," Ted read. He found this foreboding but oddly appealing. He read it aloud to Simon more than once.

And so each looked forward and planned and prepared in his own way. The time of the trip arrived, they packed their bags, they made their way to the airport, and the plane soared across the ocean to deliver them to the start of the journey.

They landed in northeastern France, in Strasbourg, where they would stay in a nice but affordable hotel and where Ted hoped to haul out his rusty college French. In the weeks leading up to the trip, and on the plane, he had fiddled around with an educational app. "This is horrible," he complained to Simon. "This isn't really learning; I can't learn the language this way." He felt righteous, vindicated, every time he spotted an error or offered a perfectly correct translation that the app rejected as wrong.

A taxi took them after some difficulty to their hotel. Once there, Ted strode up to the counter and said, uncertainly, haltingly, "Nous—avons—une—réservation." The conversation, trying for both parties, eventually led to their obtaining a keycard. He felt foolish, as though the others were indulging him, as though he were a child made to sing or dance for the adults' polite but impatient spectation. It might even, he thought, be worse later on: *what language did the denizens of this mystery nation-state speak, after all?* The app had not offered lessons in Loturian.

They had only one night in Strasbourg before beginning the pilgrimage the next day. At dinner, Simon recounted the legend, explaining that the monk and prince were held to have hailed from this region. "The prince," Ted said. "Was he the son of the king of France?"

"I don't know about that," Simon said. "I think it was something, um. Lesser than France. The story's a little unclear."

"Hmm. It's like kingdoms in fairytales. All these tiny little principalities running into each other." Ted sipped wine he did not enjoy, supposing his palate unequipped for it.

"I guess so," said Simon. He stuck a forkful of salad in his mouth.

Ted pulled a map of the route from out of his sling bag and smoothed it on the table. Simon watched Ted's index finger trace the early portion of the route. They had already gone over it many times, but the repetition reassured them both.

The next morning found them eager to begin, despite their doubts, despite the daunting nature of the journey. They wore large, ungainly backpacks and sturdy shoes purchased for the occasion. A train and then a taxi brought them to a seemingly random point in a stone road, with no markings whatsoever to distinguish its special status. The taxi driver glanced at them with confusion before driving away. Disappointed, Simon asked Ted to check the map.

"Seems a little weird, doesn't it?" Ted asked. "Shouldn't there be a sign or something?"

"Maybe it's too new?" Simon said. "This isn't some big destination—not yet, anyway." He studied the guidebook.

The men went where they believed they should go.

"So what," Ted said, "we're just going to keep walking until we reach the boat?"

"I guess," Simon said.

The first day's walk was less arduous than they'd imagined, though difficult to follow. They traversed the stone path, which eventually veered into open fields. At first, they walked hand in hand, relishing the togetherness, the adventure, their own bravery. They remained quiet, as the guidebook had advised them, to facilitate reflection and transformation. Still, Ted struggled to enjoy himself, constantly consulting the map to ensure they were following the route.

After a time, the path straightened. It was a line they could follow for hours, and he continued to trudge along it.

Simon said, "This is great. Bracing!"

Ted said, "Mm."

Each was silently imagining the legend, the young man and the very, very old who traversed mountains and fields and the coastline. In so tracing these footsteps, each felt a sort of resonance, a vague, heady, swept-away feeling. Ted did not know how to voice it, but imagining the illicit union of the men, along with their horrific, untimely deaths, added a certain pang to the mix, a sentimental anguish.

Now, walking down the stone path, he stood still and closed his eyes, keeping them shut for several seconds. This was a habit that sometimes irritated Simon. He tried to articulate something: "Those men traveled all that way, to the village, and they were killed . . ."

"Yeah," Simon said. "Convicted of witchcraft." He was a little bit ahead of Ted. He glanced back at Ted and then stopped so that the latter could catch up.

Ted had forgotten that part. "Yeah," he said and sighed. "I wonder what they actually did."

Simon frowned. "You mean, the magic? Supposedly they healed people. I think the big crime was that these outsiders were just a little different from everyone in this backwards village. Stupid."

Ted agreed.

The summer day was long and hot, and it passed slowly after the initial excitement wore off. The sun had not quite set when they arrived at the village that Ted had marked as their first day's goal. They realized it would be like this, all the onward movement and exhaustion and boredom, that it really was just walking and an awful lot of it and that, having felt the vague and heady feeling once, they may not feel it again or it may not prove worth all the effort. Neither felt prepared to express this concern out of respect for the other man's feelings.

In the little hotel, a kind of crazed exhaustion made them uncertain as to whether they should bother to eat or just go to bed. They decided to shower and regroup.

Why, wondered Ted, first as he stared at the wall while Simon showered and then as he took his turn in the cramped, poorly lit stall, *was it like that, anyway: why did they feel so tentative around each other, always dancing around the possibility of misunderstanding or of hurt?* For years they had learned to live with each other's idiosyncrasies, values, abilities, and failings, yet so often they scurried around, patently terrified to offend, oddly embarrassed when offense was unleashed. Each man wanted peace and comfort, and that's all, and mostly they could find it in each other, and sometimes not, and the not felt mysterious. Would they find peace on this trip? Ted thought not. He was beginning to fear the trip was a colossal, expensive waste of time.

They ate dinner, which was nothing much—mostly bread for two fearful vegetarians. They returned to their room and fumbled into making indifferent love. Afterward, Ted mumbled something about the next day.

"What?" Simon said.

"Oh, it's just. I think it's hit me how big of a trip this is. Like, we're just going to keep walking and walking."

"I know."

Here, the conversation ended. They relinquished themselves to sleep.

Several days followed that echoed the first. Long stretches of walking, intermittent rest, distinct but rare moments when the landscape overwhelmed and enchanted them—a response that all the subsequent walking tended to nullify. Ted or Simon would nudge the other, gently grab his arm, gesture out at the landscape. "Wow," one would say. Or "isn't that amazing." Though unable to call upon anything better, they knew these canned responses to be inadequate to the occasion.

At one point, continuing to tread the path, they came across a small body of water, a lake, upon whose surface bobbed a large goose. Simon had rarely seen geese beyond screen or page and stared at it. "It's beautiful," he told Ted. Ted thought of the logo, wondered dimly whether this might be some sort of sign. *Of what?* he thought. *That they were on the right path?*

As on the first leg of the pilgrimage, no other portion of the path featured any informative signage. Increasingly, they found themselves striking out in the middle of nowhere. Ted faced a dim thought that bloomed into a possibility: that they had descended into a *folie à deux*, that they never would get anywhere because there was nowhere to go. *But where*, he thought, *where had the literature come from?*

A couple of times here and there, they ran into someone who spoke English—other tourists, a waiter, a concierge—and they struck up tentative conversations, discussing their homes, their trips, what they had seen and done so far, but the two took time easing into the subject of their destination, explaining what it was they were doing. In truth, they had seen little, just endless roads, fields, and sky. None of their interlocutors had ever heard of the pilgrimage or the country to which they averred they were going; more than one glanced at them with puzzlement, thinking, perhaps, that this pair was a little mad.

Ted continued to worry. He kept studying not just the map but a GPS app on his phone, pinching the image on the screen to zoom into where Loturia was supposed to be. The digital stretch of pale blue water transfixed him. It was supposed to be there, and it was not. What would they do when they traveled the length of the road and ran into the northern coast, where there should be a peninsula but where, Ted was convinced, nothing would await them?

They moved on. The days jumbled together, a haze of summer heat, clothes gone sodden with sweat, endless thirst, and dullness. They could only take in so much landscape and, once sated, barely processed it at all.

Two weeks in, Simon grew testy. "Our brains are getting pickled," he said. "All this heat." Ted kept seeing geese in flight, wings stretched in the blue sky that evoked for him the water. *The water was there*, he thought, *and Loturia wasn't.*

He thought: *if they were geese, if they were there at all and their brains had not grown pickled.*

The hotel they stayed in that night featured on the ground floor a small dining area, where they ate eggy pasta and sipped beers. It was a small, close, and hot room, the air stale from cooking. A young and attractive waiter led them to a booth in the corner away from the room's other diners. After a time, a woman sat down who broached a conversation. She had black graying hair and wore several fussy-looking layers of clothing, too many, Ted thought, for the season. She said, "So where are you two headed?"

Simon sighed. "We are on a pilgrimage," he said. "We are tracing the route of a monk who was burned at the stake. The route ends in a country called Loturia, which apparently cannot be found on normal maps."

"Oh!" she said. "I've heard of it. My sister knew a man once who came from there. It's not an easy place to reach. It's a little"—she paused—"It's different."

Both Simon and Ted sat up as she spoke. Simon said, "Different how?"

She looked uncomfortable or evasive. "I really don't know much—I never met the man my sister knew, and I have never been there. I don't know anything else." And then she shrugged. "I'm going home tomorrow," she said. "I've had enough of travel."

After that, the chitchat dried up. She soon departed, drink in hand, leaving the men to their beers and empty plates.

As they were about to leave, the waiter stopped and spoke quietly to Simon: "If you have already decided to go, you might as well be there already."

In bed, they spoke about the waiter. "What the hell was he talking about?" Simon asked. He was changing into his pajamas.

Ted raised his hands in perplexity.

Simon slid into bed and said, "This trip was a bad idea." He turned the light out and flipped over.

At some point, in the dark, Simon said, "By following this route, we'll become enlightened? Isn't that our destination?"

Ted, not asleep, said, "Something like that." Eventually, and poorly, they slept.

The days went on, and their moods flipped between sour and bored and a little hopeful. Each of them was stubborn and felt that they could not now abandon the trip, must see it through to the end. This was true despite Simon's growing anxiety that there was no destination and that no enlightenment lay in wait for them; despite Ted's fear that they had, together, lost their minds.

They now avoided conversation with others, not that they saw so many others, and stuck to watching the sky and the water and waiting until they reached the ship that would take them to the village.

Near the coast, they found that a glimpse of the sea enlivened them a little. They felt near to the end. And, in the end, what? Some heartening of spirit, some imagined connection with a pair of long-dead men would persuade them that it had all been worth it. What is a pilgrimage for? They imagined it was to pay respect, respect to history and the dead, to stoke spirituality or obtain some ephemeral scrap of meaning. And would they? With every step taken, every drop of sweat exuded on the surface of the skin, one more piece of the self was shed. A greater meaning eluded them, and they were chasing it, would not stop chasing it until they were there. They would approach the heart of who they were. Simon continued to cling to this belief. But there, at their destination, in a village historically devoted to treating visitors with suspicion, hostility, and worse, Ted could hardly believe they would find anything that might induce transformation.

Along the water they trekked until they found a harbor. The harbor was marked on their map. Until they were there, until they saw a ship before them, floating on the water, neither had fully believed it would be there. Ted, for one, had come to expect to find more water and a coast that simply stopped, proving that Loturia did not exist. It stunned him, a little, to think that this could be here and somehow finagle its way out of history, slip past the watchful eyes of those who write it. The monk and the prince had come here and done the same; they confronted the harbor and walked out of time, it seemed to him, journeying farther into their own dooms.

He looked out at the sea, which he found to be wine-dark. He understood, here and now, what the Greeks meant, that the sea could resemble wine not in hue but in opacity. It was dark and thickly swirling. There is no such thing as objectivity; we have only the partial view. Reality is fluid, malleable, as much as the sea, at times dark and at others light; sometimes the light pierces it and it is transparent, whereas at other times it churns impenetrably.

The monk and the prince had not, it turns out, made it far past the border of Loturia, though they could not have known it beforehand. Unless the monk had: if he could see past and future, he might have known his fate, the knowledge that he and his companion would soon meet such exquisite hostility. Ted thought that he must not have; he must, on that count at least, have been lying, or his powers were limited. Surely he did not know.

The ship halted at another coast, and Simon and Ted ventured into Loturia. Above, the sun pierced a hole in the sky, a radiant eye within the endless searing blue. They could hear at the distant fringes of awareness a low droning sound, which might have been a kind of chant. Nobody greeted them, nothing marked their entrance save for the ship, and another goose that Ted saw overhead. He tugged at Simon's arm and pointed.

Ted thought to pull up his GPS app, zooming into their current location. It showed a small dot floating in pale blue. Their location was not there; they were off the map.

It had long been Ted's practice to close his eyes and seek a canvas of pure white. It was a strategy to calm himself, attain a state of focus: he considered it seeking, not imagining, and he did consider what he saw with closed eyes as a canvas, cluttered with color and texture, and bit by bit every inch of it was painted over, so that all he saw was a vista of white. Or not a vista, and not a canvas either, both of which are wrong, for they imply some distance, a position from which he observed the white but was not of it. What he sought when he sought the pure white was total immersion or, better, the effacement of himself into that state of purity. This goal typically proved impossible. He tried it now at Loturia's edge and, failing, opened his eyes and glanced at his phone, at the dot in a place it should not be.

They were off the map, yet the land unrolled before them. They proceeded to the village. This did not take long. They had not realized the village would appear so quickly, but there it was, a cluster of small stone buildings that must have been built centuries back, perhaps even the very same buildings that the monk and the prince encountered.

And there it was: The skin of the world fell loose as by sharp and skillful knifework, and something seeped out. It had been thus loosening throughout the whole trip. The world at last slithered out of it, shed like snakeskin.

There was nobody here. The houses—it was obvious—were empty. The houses might have been a film set, all lined up in tidy rows, centered on a square prettily paved in a mosaic of multicolored stones, which were scuffed and fractured but mostly intact. Absolutely nothing was audible apart from that same low droning.

A fountain stood in the middle of the square, emptied of water. Cracks splayed across the bottom of its basin. In the center of the fountain danced a set of carved figures that Ted did not recognize—mammals of some indistinct variety, along with one that might have been a goose. *The native fauna of Loturia*, he thought. At the center of the figures rose a very thick spout, but its crown was cracked. It seemed to Ted unusually thick—large enough to hide in.

The droning echoed louder near the fountain. He approached it, stepped into the basin, and climbed the strange statues. He reached the spout and peered into its jagged mouth. Looking down, inside of it, he saw a bird's eye view of a town, bustling, much larger than this one, yet—given the fountain in the middle, which he could see even from this vantage—possibly the same place or a version of it. Its miniscule citizens walked down narrow streets that appeared no larger than Ted's fingers.

Startled, he pulled his head away. He looked again and saw now a village, possibly medieval, much closer in appearance to the place in which he now stood. He could see tiny people, fewer than the last time, going about their daily business, oblivious to the eye that watched from far above.

Ted again removed his head from the broken spout. He wondered if the view would always change. No two people saw the same thing; they couldn't. No two sets of eyes, or no two sets of glimpses from the same eyes, would find the same view down the spout, and no two minds would agree on what it meant.

Ted wondered what the monk had seen. He wondered what the monk had caused to be seen, if the accusations lobbed at him proved true. What sorcery was it that had visited this place?

Simon was by now far off, looking at the houses, perhaps, or a person, or any sort of trace of or memorial to the monk and the prince. Ted saw a flash of movement in his peripheral vision, turned, and saw Simon dart around a corner. He stood in place, sliding his backpack to the ground and digging through it until he found the literature he had ordered to prepare for the trip.

He found the brochure and pulled it out, but its pages, unfolding in his hands, proved to be completely different. The same shape and size, the brochure featured none of the pictures, none of the breathless text that had incited them to go on the pilgrimage. It retained the logo, if it was a logo: an elaborate goose that curled around itself in a circle. But the document consisted now of many lines of text in faded ink. He did not know whether it was the document that had changed or himself; he might have been, now, a new observer.

He read, "There once was a monk who spent a century alone in a grotto, devoted to prayer . . ." He stood still and read every word, the whole story of the monk who emerged from his grotto and traveled with the prince to a distant country, where they found death—and not only death—and when he was done he flung the paper to the ground and sought to look for Simon.

It did not take long, for in the meantime Simon had exhausted his own search. He sat on the fountain's far side, cross-legged like a child. He was gazing at the creatures in the center of the fountain.

Simon stood up when he saw Ted approaching. The men embraced, arms wrapped around each other in the sticky heat, and then they drew apart. They did not speak.

They saw the pyre, which stood near the fountain. They walked toward it and took their places. Piles of desiccated wood had burned long ago, right here. Fires, once extinguished, left trails of smoke that moved skyward, dissipating into the air. Rain came and soaked the wood, which took its time drying in the blistering heat. The pyre remained, perfectly intact. Nobody had ever disturbed it; none had ever cleaned it up or moved it. Here, too, the men found partial perspectives: the view of the pyre and from it.

As they stood at the pyre, each man imagined he could feel a nonexistent fire's heat, its scorching along his skin. The drone or chant grew louder until it seemed a force that could wrap them up, surround them, and each grew convinced he heard a kind of prayer, a voice or voices raised in mournful ululation, as though imploring some unreal being who likely could not hear. Each closed his eyes and opened them, looking on absent faces, the faces of those who clamored to watch him burn, but he did not burn; he did not burn but felt a prickling heat across the surface of his body, somehow distant but close, just inches away. They stood there for a long time.

III

The Breath Before the Cut

~ *Megan Lee Beals*

The ghost watches Nia's hands as she smooths its muslin against the dress form. The form, with its shining metal skeleton and thick tweed skin, is as foreign to the ghost as every other splendid shining thing in the tower it woke to. Nia says that a thousand years have passed since the ghost's death, and yet, work remains the same. The skilled are used and discarded by the wealthy.

Nia's scissors are ready in her other hand, the sharp blades sliding apart, like a mouth breathing open just before a kiss.

Nia's eyes meet the ghost's. Dark and beautiful, not asking permission, but hesitating still. The ghost blinks slowly at her. Its mummified lids flutter over her clear and living eyes, and it gives a nod.

This is not the first desecration Nia has committed for fashion, but it is the first time the ghost stands over her shoulder to watch.

Nia used to work in museums, in restoration, but when she cut into The Turkish Gown and remade the ancient gem incrusted thing into a suit for one of Hollywood's royals, she became infamous in the world of fashion.

The sort of wealth that hired her now liked to trade in novel transgressions, their money so immeasurable that expenditure wasn't about the purchase so much as it signified their singular taste.

The Bog Muslin was a thousand years old. Its very fibers had gone extinct five hundred years ago, along with the skill to spin its fine cotton filament into thread. It was not the oldest example of cotton muslin, but it was by far the largest intact piece, and this bolt of fabric came with its very own ghost.

It was described as a presence, a heavy cold that settled around the heart and lungs of any who got near the fabric. Something Nia could fake with a drafty room and a warbling reverence put into her voice when she unveiled her work for the superstitious rich man who hired her. Nia did not expect to find it sitting on the crate, with its mummified lips pulled back in a perpetual smile.

"I'm the artist," she told it that first morning, with the same hardened authority she forced her voice into whenever she spoke to a new client, because the thing unnerved her, and she knew that any sign of weakness in her line of work would be her undoing. "I'm going to cut the fabric."

The ghost made a pathetic little whine through its desiccated lips, and any fear Nia might have held folded into pity. The ghost was ugly. Death pulled its lips away from overlong teeth and sucked its flesh hard against the skull. The skin was stained a greenish brown from the bog it had sat in for a thousand years, and the hair, stringy, black, knotted, fell in clumps around its shoulders. It seemed unfair that its spirit was trapped in the same decay as the body that was dredged up from the bog.

"What's your name?"

The ghost shrugged. Such a casual motion for a manifested jump scare. Nia looked into its eyes and found them ordinary. The whites unstained, the iris's dark and rich and lovely, like the eyes of a living woman trapped inside the mask of her death.

"Did you weave it?" asked Nia, because even if she forgot her own name, Nia would know her own work.

The ghost nodded. Nia smiled, silently seizing her victory. Nia would not need its name. Its spirit was woven into the fabric the same way she made herself in her dresses. There was not an artist in the world that did not leave ghosts in their work.

The ghost has not breathed in a thousand years, and yet it draws a sharp breath as Nia's scissors slip up beneath the fabric, so sharp that gravity itself would make the cut if the fabric had any weight at all. But when the ghost woke to this modern world, in a beautiful tower so stark and gleaming that it seemed to be carved of glass, it found that the wonders of the modern world had forgotten the humble wonder of its work. No one could make fabric that felt like spring dew on the skin, that moved like air itself. It did not matter that the bolt of muslin was stained with the ghost's death, with the centuries they spent entombed together.

When Nia explained that she was making a dress, the ghost felt its heart crack with joy that its work might finally

*see light. That joy crumbled into sorrow when Nia assured
it that the dress will be made for another.*

*The rich man will be here soon to pass judgement on
the dress, but Nia has been pacing around the fabric for a
week. She has nothing to show him for his expense, and no
matter how much the world has changed in the last thousand years, the inherent danger in defying a rich man has
remained the same.*

Nia spent days sketching before she dared to drape the
muslin on the dress form. She was afraid that the rough
tweed might pull at the fabric, that it would crumble to
dust if she touched it, but the ghost's work was preserved
in the bog. Its weave remained strong.

After surmounting the considerable hurdle of moving
the muslin out of its box, Nia was at a loss for how to
sew it. The finest thread that the modern world had to
offer stood out like a giraffe among horses when she set it
against the fabric.

She informed the rich man that she would make that a
feature of the dress. Seams would be made with embroi-
dery, miniscule flowers chasing up the hem, impercep-
tible to all but the closest observers. His new wife's new
dress would be an intimate, possessive thing, the design
meant for his eyes alone.

She breathed a sigh when she got off the phone, grate-
ful that he bought her vision, and that vision bought her
more time with the fabric.

The ghost reached for her with its horrible claw of a hand, and the bones passed through Nia like a cold mist. Nia jumped back, her mouth pulled in horror, but she schooled it away as the ghost bowed its head in apology.

"Do all dressmakers live like queens?" rasped the ghost, its voice like a breeze through a broken window. The ghost's perpetual grin was even wider. The warm brown eyes completely gone behind the crinkle of its papery skin.

"This isn't my home."

The rich man placed Nia in his tower with every luxury she could think to ask for the moment she signed over her skills. She fished a compressed fruit bar out of her pocket and unwrapped it. Unfortunately, in considering luxuries, she forgot to ask for a well stocked kitchen.

"You are a caged bird, then."

"Something like that. Singing for supper." She looked around the stark open plan loft. White and chrome and leather. The ghost was the liveliest thing in it.

"It's a pretty big song, though," said Nia. "I just have to sing once, then I'll have every supper taken care of."

"How many?"

"What?"

The ghost leaned close. Death frosted the white leather couch Nia sat upon. "It is easy to promise the rest of someone's life, if you only consider that life while it is useful." The ghost ran its long leathery fingers over its neck, stopping at the torn flesh of her throat. Not torn. It was cut.

Nia's eyes narrowed. "They're not going to kill me. That's crazy. I have a contract. There's a paper trail."

"I was promised safety, too," said the ghost.

"I'm sorry." It was a small thing to say, in the face of death, but Nia could not stop herself from saying it.

"He is nothing, now. And I am in a tower, with a beautiful princess." The ghost's lips pulled further back in a horrific smile. "Who seeks to bind my spirit forever to a beautiful dress."

Nia hesitates. Her hands, usually so steady, are tremoring. She's going to ruin the fabric. The ghost presses close to her, enough to frost her eyelashes with its presence, and Nia draws her scissors away.

No.

The ghost forces its withered claw against Nia's warm hand and pushes until it clicks itself into her bones. They are similar enough in spirit that it is like stepping into one's own home, if all the furniture was moved half-a-span to the right. The ghost draws Nia's hand away from the dress form and tests her muscles by opening the scissors once, twice . . . beautiful. The glass tower is a cold place, and its miracles tarnished quickly in the span of a week, but a good pair of scissors is worth a thousand years in the bog. The ghost grins and brings Nia's hand back to the dress, but Nia chokes out a little sound, and the ghost finds tears in her eyes.

"Stop."

The ghost pulls away from her and hides behind the dress form.

"I can't."

"I'll help you," says the ghost.

"I don't want to."

That had been clear from their first meeting, but the ghost had thought Nia past her hesitance.

"What if it hurts you?"

"I'm dead."

"Well then . . . maybe I don't want you to go."

"Then keep me." The ghost settles its spirit into the muslin and shivers all the pins until they rain down to the floor. It sweeps the muslin off the dress form and drapes it around Nia's shoulders. "We can leave anytime."

"It's his tower," Nia reminds it.

"And he will be here soon to view the dress," says the ghost. Nia waited too long, and the rich man's disappointment was imminent.

She nods. Nia will have to admit to her inability to cut the muslin, and she will be thrown out of his society with nothing but the ire of the world she left behind. The masses never forgave her for The Turkish Gown. "I have nothing to show him."

The ghost smiles. It reaches for her hand and grasps it tightly when its given. "So lets make something," says the ghost. It presses further into Nia's skin. Spectral bone scrapes lovingly against her muscle and slots easily into place as Nia accepts the ghost's presence into herself. As the ghost tucks its face behind her ear, it whispers gently, "He wanted a haunted dress. Let's make him want an exorcism."

PAGE of WANDS.

Lepid Little Lies

~ Pen Anderson

Echoing off the glass, concrete, and asphalt of Midtown Manhattan is a slow whooshing mixed with a repetitive zipper rhythm. A roar like a flame-belching top fuel dragster pulling organ pipes over a highway rumblestrip at two-hundred miles-per-hour—a tornado chasing behind. The decibels of pressure confuse wind with sound, buffeting and nearly deafening Kipling as he stands at the corner of Lexington and 48th, looking towards the sky.

Across the intersection, the dim morning light highlights a giant ermine moth hovering some ten stories up. Its wingspan the width of a city block. A three-story abdomen hangs nearly to the ground as wings gyrate in-place. Hairy fringed wingtips graze the buildings to either side. The gusts of their beating synchronized with pulses of the rumblestrip grind.

Dust swirls in the air all around them.

He can feel his heart picking up, his armpits suddenly damp. Kipling can't remember the last panic attack that hit this hard. After a few seconds—or minutes, as Kipling felt it—of looking eye-to-oh-so-many-eyes, the hovering moth twists its thorax. Thin, alabaster legs reach out with hooked claws over padded arolia to put six footholds on the closest office building. The pervasive cacophony ceases the moment the wings still, and a muffled ringing floods into the sudden aural void. The moth tucks in a bit, coming to rest like a glittering avenue banner over the street. Its head to the sky, subway train antennae probe well over the twenty-story building's roof.

Legs twitch a bit to rain more broken glass and concrete onto a steel awning poking out above the building's doors. Most of the street is dark in the shadow of the morning; but, the August sun crests rooftops to illuminate the moth directly and reflect moon-like light in a diffuse, rectangular beam through the air. A downy mantle of elongated entomological hairs covers the moth's neck and shoulders in a regal crest over a speckled fur robe. Kipling's rolling gaze comes to halt on those robe-like wings—draped and folded around its body. Hickory brown voids as wide as his own head draw him in—devouring his attention. Peripheral scales glow in glares of milky silver and hyaline rainbows against the dull gray high-rise.

Beneath the moth, a line of people streams out of the building. They've come out prepared with umbrellas to avoid the raining debris. Their expressions are bored—ignoring the colossal cryptid resting directly above them. Spending their attention on anything else.

Kipling forces himself to turn away and pulls out his phone. His hands shake as he types out a message to let his boss know he's taking a sick day. After pocketing the phone, he takes a couple deliberate inhales, holds, then exhales slowly—a ritual he learned from his therapist. As he sighs, the tremble slows. Looking around now, no one is within a block of him. He's completely alone. He does not count the impossible yponomeutid still twitching in the corner of his vision.

Kipling proceeds to walk toward the subway with the dignity of someone who is certainly not still hallucinating an insect that could pick up a school bus.

Each step away from that kaiju obsession brings a fraction more calm. Though the memory of the moth's grinding cacophony sticks as an earworm. He distracts himself by taking exaggerated, silly steps over each crease in the sidewalk. Gray dust coats the pavement as he walks. Mica-flecked, it sometimes glitters just barely before crunching beneath his shoes. Leaving barely visible footprints in the layers, Kipling's steps proceed more deliberately.

The street around him remains mostly deserted. Some of the recent evacuees are strolling under their umbrellas, but most have scattered completely. A food cart stands unattended. Cups emitting a faint sour smell rest on outdoor bistro tables. A taxi sits with its rear door open, but no one enters nor emerges. Kipling doesn't consider any of it though—his head down, eyes on the dusty pavement—out of sight, out of mind.

Arriving at the green and yellow globes of the subway entrance, Kipling feels safer. Something about enclosed spaces, concrete and steel between him and the sky—he cuts the thought short and jogs down the stairs, mentally revising his upcoming day. Maybe he'll finally clean out his refrigerator.

A few people are down here, too, moving between stations underground; but, not as many as Kipling would expect to be commuting this morning. Individuals and sparse groups move through the pedways and platforms. No staff to be seen. The turnstiles are broken and the accessibility gate stands propped open. A taped, handwritten sign on it reads: TEMPORARY SERVICE ADJUSTMENT. Inattentive, Kipling walks through the gate and beyond.

At the platform he finds a vaguely bench-shaped beam to lean against—a hostile, unreclinable replacement for a bench. Looking at the few people who are around—some pop-a-squat still, most moving with nervous intent—inspires in Kipling a sense of the uncanny before he closes his eyes and takes another deliberate breath.

The sensation of space around him expands a bit as he focuses on the feeling of cool metal through the butt of his jeans, the distant hum of ventilation systems, the familiar smell of subway: mold, urine, and musk. A New Yorker's cure for homesickness. Grounded by disgust.

A puff of dust ejects from a ventilation grate overhead and drifts down to settle on his shoulders. Kipling brushes it away without looking at it, but feels some distinct grains poke the back of his fingers. Less than conscious, a sub-tectonic anger amplifies into a physical tremble. Probably just low blood sugar. Did he eat yet?

"You're covered in it, you know."

Kipling's eyes startle open. The speaker is standing a few feet ahead of him—enough not to be crowding. She's wearing a clean jacket, pleated blouse, and slacks that calm him. Among the few vagrants currently at the platform, her suit, tightly pulled hair, and thin-framed glasses stands out as overly sophisticated. Her old-fashioned looks inspire nostalgia in him. He almost questions why he doesn't see anyone so professional, dynamic, and purpose-driven in the city anymore.

"Excuse me?" he responds.

"The dust, see?" She waves her hand about, completing the gesture to encompass him. "It's all over you like craft herpes after a dancer's orgy."

Kipling follows where she's pointing, looking down at himself to see more glitter than dust on his hands, legs, torso. She's right. It is all over him.

"Why? Uh, did I get bombed? Is this an ad?" He asks, but his confusion quickly shifts to doubt. He follows up, "What is it?" Kipling's voice strains on that last question despite himself. It feels both pointless and dangerous, like he shouldn't be asking at all.

"Scales," she states, matter-of-fact.

He loses sight for a moment, feels the blood drop out of his face, and subsequently retches. Raising his hands to his mouth stops nothing. Kipling violently ejects his breakfast through his fingers, all over the woman in front of him. He had something in him, apparently.

She jumps back, but it's already too late. There's a vague orangeness spattered on her suit, from belly down to knees, already creeping through her blouse and dropping small chunks to the floor. She lets out a sing-songy "Fuuuuck!", drawing more attention from the platform residents—those who weren't already reacting to the vomit itself.

Revulsion and fascination in equal measure among their faces, a passerby walks closer to the tracks in avoidance. The squatters watch without shame, their expressions suggesting this is, by far, the most interesting thing they've seen on the subway today.

"I'm sorry," Kipling states with a rasp. "I have an anxiety disorder."

"Clearly." She quips, before politely saying, "It's ok, I'm an Easer." She peels the damp blouse away from her belly with one hand, while she walks around Kipling to corral him with the other. "Let's go somewhere else," she says as she leads him back upstairs, off the platform. Her tone is inviting, as if wearing someone's puke was just another form of introduction.

The onlookers give them plenty of space to move on.

Kipling steps slowly along with her, but slips out of awareness. As far as he's concerned, he's not even thinking. Eyes forward, but not seeing, he retreats without leaving.

A rumble is barely audible in the tunnels back below them.

The kind new companion guides Kipling through the pedway between stations. Her hand remains steady on his elbow, neither pushing nor pulling, just providing direction. Kipling follows automatically, distantly wondering if puking on a stranger is how one gets recruited by a secret society, or a cult. Will he be expected to accept a similar gastric gift in exchange? Spit-shake on it?

Oblivious to Kipling's unspoken questions, she pseudo-replies with a forced positivity, "Yeah! I'm just going to keep talking. I get the feeling like you're . . . You're processing some pretty big things right now, and, well . . . I mean, see . . . It's OK, we all handle it differently. I don't know that I believe in this whole 'Go along; get along. What's done is done and nothing to do.' Never have . . . Been an Easer for, uhhh . . . Well . . . In the before-times we just had cook-offs, fundraisers, soup kitchen meetups, see? Some folks still do all that, but . . . It's both smaller and much bigger at the same time . . . Compassion and charity . . ." Her inflections gradually lose energy.

Kipling clears his throat at the last pause. "Hey, thanks," he says as he stops walking and looks at her. He's fully back in the now. "I really appreciate your care and all. Really, really sorry about puking on you. I'm Kipling, can I ask your name?" He extends his hand, then remembers the vomit, and awkwardly waves instead.

With a warm smile and a hand to her heart, "June. So pleased to meet you, Kipling." June glances down to the orange on her and says in a resigned, yet cheerful tone, "This will be OK. I was going to a job interview. But, yeah. I'm going to have to ghost 'em."

Kipling looks back along their path saying, "I should really just go home." Home, where he can shower, where there are no strangers covered in his breakfast, and where he is much less likely to see building-sized moths.

"Mhmm. Is that where you were heading?" June replies while resuming their walk through the pedway, approaching another station.

"I was headed to work, then . . ." Kipling trails off, losing his track of memory before continuing. "I called in sick." He chuckles to himself about the ironic lie, since he did, in fact, throw up soon afterward.

June nods slowly. "First time?"

"First time what? Lying to my boss? Puking suddenly in the subway? Oh, no, I'm diagnosed. Panic has a way of emptying me in various ways."

"First time seeing her in-person, I mean. You already said you have a disorder." June's pace picks up slightly as she leads them through another open station gate and down the stairs to the platform.

Kipling awkwardly weaves around a support beam at the base of the stairs as June speeds ahead. Catching up to her he wobbles a bit more. In his selective attention, he had overlooked the people walking on and along the rails, lights from under the platform casting shadows up tall against the tunnel walls. For the major length of the platform, Kipling had imagined the outline of a train car around their projections—could have sworn he heard the squeal and spark of breaks, but there are no trains here. Just umbrella-carrying pedestrians getting by on their own power.

A few free-standing step-ladders join the platform to the tracks here. Makeshift staircases. Kipling and June use them to get down and hop along the tracks southbound before Kipling reaches to check his phone. In another mental flight from the here-and-now, he wonders if this alternative route will make him late for work today.

Into the tunnel, illumination is provided by a motley of rope LEDs, work lights, and floor lamps with RGB bulbs. Long extension cords are patched between power strips—some strung up on the conduits overhead, some standing on posts and tripods. June doesn't seem surprised by this makeshift pedestrian thoroughfare. Even Kipling isn't really surprised, just confused about what he's trying not to see.

"What are we doing?" Kipling is still following, keeping up with the faster pace as they walk unconcernedly next to the third rail.

"Taking the 5 Express downtown."

"The train is out of service." Kipling says in a quavering voice betraying his uncertainty. He glances around for any MTA employees who might enforce whatever rule prohibits pedestrians on the tracks, but finds no one. He looks at his phone to check the time, but returns it to his pocket without really seeing what it said.

June laughs and lilts, "Yeeees?" Sarcastic.

He opens his mouth and holds it open for a while, not quite able to articulate what is wrong here. He commutes daily, but in trying to recall the specifics of yesterday's ride home he just can't. Kipling considers that, in his own defense, he also doesn't remember what he had for breakfast today, in spite of looking at its current form wrapped around June's slacks. His route wouldn't have taken him this way anyhow, so he figures it's just a context dependent memory issue. Go back north, and he could remind himself. Right?

"We can hoof it back up on the street if you prefer," June offers. "But, judging from the shock I found you in, you probably don't prefer." Her tone suddenly shifts to something more casual, diverting, "How long have you been in the city?"

"Born and raise—!" Kipling's response jumps high and cuts off as he rams his shin into the sharp, metal corner of a control box protruding from the floor. The pain is clarifying, almost comforting in its banality.

June stops for him and looks down to a new slash in his jeans, a cut visible and bleeding behind it. "Oh shit, sorry." She approaches, making to crouch and look closer, but holds back.

Kipling turns from June and hisses as he takes another step, feeling his cut stretch and open a bit as he moves.

"I didn't bring any first-aid," June stands back.

"I'll be fine, just let me walk through it." Kipling limps forward some more, getting ahead of June with the stoicism of someone who would rather forget the pain than treat the injury. Every once in a while taking nervous glances back along the rails.

"Born and raised, huh?" she says, her eyes narrowing, "I'm going to get angry now. Why are you still acting like such a tourist? I just don't really appreciate the rhetoric. We don't have to pretend, just let each other be, right?" June's pace slows down behind Kipling, "I think it's why I'm out of work, see." She sighs, "No one's gotta agree with me, but can't we just talk about it? What's wrong with venting?" The anger she tries to evoke never really comes forth; instead, sad resolve. "Can't we just say what's real and on our minds? How can anyone get tired of that? How can you live your life without expressing it?"

Kipling stops his limping while noticing a bit of glitter in the worklights.

June, uninterrupted, continues, "I was miserable. We are all so miserable. Masking all the time. All. Of. The. Time. Why?" Her voice rises with each repetition.

"Because it isn't real." Kipling finds himself replying.

"Damn right, it ain't" June agrees, missing the point, but finally fired up, "It's just so fucking weird. Five years ago, you tell me a giant moth would come to New York? Naw. No way! Today? A star-man in fuckin' Louisiana? Yeah! Robocop in Detroit? Yeah! Except, no. Just the fucking murder bot." Her fire continues, "I understand, I get it. I do. In the face of such fucked-uppity, how can you even begin to talk straight about it? Get-Along-Sam says 'Don't worry, live your days. What you can't change don't try to.'" She delivers the quote in a drawl, then takes a moment to breathe before saying, "I grew up looking up, looking forward, working towards hope, progress, rationality. We had *Star Trek!*"

Stunned by her own excitement, June tries to affect a dismissive tone, ". . . and Asimov, and Chambers, yeah. And Weir. Plenty of great, equitable, probable paths. Am I making any sense?"

They come to a stop facing each other, standing on adjacent ties.

"Oh, I dunno. I know *Star Trek*. Are you saying something about aliens?" Kipling doesn't let himself stand on the wounded leg for long. He steps onward still in some pain, with less of a limp.

June's brow furrows in deep perplexity. She follows along with Kipling, but a half a minute passes before she answers, "No, I don't think so. I'm not really sure on that one really, but not right now. I just mean that at some point—even before the moth, really. The people with all the power and money showed us that they didn't believe in any of those visions, like *Star Trek*—and I think they might have even, like, rejected Gandhi."

Kipling is both riveted and losing focus on what June is saying. He continues walking without interrupting her.

June continues, "They had already decided on another kind of truth. They showed us that they were preparing for this shit and gunning to make all of this happen. That it had to happen to justify all their hoarding and prep."

He knows what she's talking about, but he's still trying to figure out how it relates to his hallucination. She talks about the moth as if it's not a product of his own panic. He stops walking again, seeing another glint.

June stops with him, but goes on venting, "I guess I always worried, too. That—in spite of really buying into hope and solarpunk, community and inclusion—that we'd still get stepped on by all that cyberpunk and horror, paranoia and insanity.

"I didn't expect literal giant animals, bigoted robots, and dynastic trade conglomerates replacing the services traditionally reserved for governments. That sounds like a mouthful, I know, but all of these vast horrors . . . Even the bureaucratic ones." June takes an overdue breath before she wraps up this eruption of science-fiction resentments. "It's not just Toho, Tanaka. It gets even bigger, more existential. It's all just so much bigger than all of us. It's H.P. Lovecraft and Philip K. Dick. It always has been and always gonna be god-damned Lovecraft and Dick."

Kipling delivers a deadpan retort, "I was still thinking along the lines of *Animal Farm*."

June's explosion of awkward laughter expands through the tunnels.

Kipling doesn't laugh, but he does note that June's outburst doesn't resonate as brightly in the direction he's facing. Towards the glint. This isn't a fleck of mica or scale. This is the crawling gleam of a silken line.

June turns to look along with Kipling, following the aim of his scrutiny. Just ahead is the last work light as far as they can see. But that's not what they're looking at. Sheets of webbing stretch from arch to rail, skirting the walls, completely covering the tunnel ahead. Hyper-planar tapestries at sharp angles to each other fence off a cellular labyrinth that obscures a complete darkness within.

"This is OK," June states.

Kipling stumbles over his words, trying to reconcile what he sees to what June is saying and to what he believes. She isn't giving him enough to be confident. "It's OK to . . . be so . . . ? dark? You have a flashlight?"

"Well, yeah, we have phones. But, we also have another route." Pulling out her phone and switching on its flashlight, June redirects Kipling's attention to their right. There's a gap in the light brick wall just past where the last lamp stands, before the webs get thick. "This is our stop. I know I said we were taking the express, but we gotta hop off early to transfer to another line. It's just a little detour."

"Where?" Kipling also pulls out his phone and lights up the ground in front of him.

June jogs forward and hops through the vacant doorway. Beyond the wall she shines the light of her phone up, brightening a wide area around them. But, without the network of extension cables on this side, there are no running lamps. While he feels lucky that he isn't seeing any webs on this side, the cold light of both of their phones quickly falls off into darkness, leaving both north and south in complete mystery.

She leads them across a few more sets of tracks, ducking under and weaving between steel supports, before hopping from rail up onto the yellow gripped edge of a station platform.

Kipling's limp is gone by now, though he still feels the tension on his shin with each stride. Rather than hop, he lifts and rolls himself up onto the platform, gets up from his knees, and eventually catches up with June, who is shining her phone at deliberately staged fragments of antique mosaic-tiled walls.

Embossing each of the wall fragments, heraldic eagles grasp starry-edged shields emblazoned with the number 14. On the station's true wall, behind the excised museum pieces, their lights pick out UNION SQUARE.

June beams at her own cleverness, "14th Street, Union Square, see?"

Kipling searches the platform with his own light, glancing over blue and red pillars, stairways, another platform past a few more sets of track. Something disturbs the dust from the ceiling as he looks around, spiking his vigilance.

"We should be able to get through on this side. Get on the 'Q' or whatever."

"To where?"

"We're goin' to City Hall! We're gonna get our grievances heard!" June's laugh waxes maniacal as she raises her chin and puffs out her chest, her gait transforming into a march. "You've been in the city how long again?" June looks back to ask.

"My whole life." Kipling answers.

"And you still wait to catch the train downtown?"

Kipling hesitates, "I never come downtown except to get to Brooklyn."

June guffaws, "Oho, you fancy Upper East Side boy, are you?"

"Hamilton Heights."

"Mmm—"

Kipling, anticipating a critique of gentrification, snaps, "Yeah, it's come up, but I got my place from my parents when they passed. I'm from here, there. I rent there, and I can barely afford it on my own. They didn't leave me much else besides the apartment."

June guides Kipling along the extended platform, out of the station, continuing on the ledge above the tracks. Kipling might be catching more silken gleams on the edge of their flashlight range. Maybe some movement. Did he see a train go past? He shines his light, but across the grid of girders, shadows are cast in all directions, and he can't be sure of anything. If it was a train silently rolling along between him and the silk, it was a small one.

"Well, you're not a landlord, at least." June looks back at Kipling again, keeping her light shining ahead. "You can save your battery," she says with a nod to his phone.

He stops to fumble off the light. "What happened? Why are the trains still out?" Kipling feels his voice tighten.

June heaves a sigh before saying, "You're serious? You're so precious. You've been here forever, but you've been living under a rock. Have you left that apartment since you were born, dude?"

Kipling's sight dims and his step shuffles. The echoing grind from under his shoes evocative of another song he's trying to forget.

"Sorry," June says, "I forgot you said you have a thing. I shouldn't be so . . ."

Kipling fights against passing out and takes a hard step, forcing his shin-gash to throb and tear the scab a bit. Another drip of blood races down between previously streaked leg hairs. The psychological retreat halted by physiological distraction. "Can you please go on, actually?"

June blinks, continues, "Alright, well you saw the moth, right? Three years ago it came here, showed up here, grew here, maybe. But, suddenly we had an invasive species like you never seen."

Kipling doesn't want to listen, but also won't let himself focus on anything other than June's words and her silhouette bobbing with the light beaming ahead of her.

"Moth didn't do much to folks, but fly around, kicking up dust devils and breaking a few windows. Though there was one window . . . ugh." June swallows.

This is feeling less like news and more like a story he's getting tired of hearing. Familiar, almost unimportant. But, he's starting to realize it might be the most important.

"Well, I guess this mom was walking with her kid on the edge of Central Park and like . . . Well, the moth knocked loose a window on one of the buildings which caught the air just right, flew across the street and chopped the mom in half, or decapitated her or some shit. Kid was right there. Fuck. I can't imagine what that kid is doing today."

Kipling remembers some things his therapist had said suddenly reframed with context—Denial is disconnection. It puts you in a different world from everyone else. Finding himself emotionally exhausted and deeply empathizing, he doesn't press for history again. Not just yet.

The two of them walk in silent gloom. Kipling can't stop picturing the scene June implanted. Super-imposed with his more recent vision of the moth. She said out loud that he saw it? Was that the first time? That's what she was asking? No. He's been having this same hallucination for how long? Has it been three years?

After about a mile of them both letting their minds wander, Kipling watches June's halo and the platform between them—not looking at the silk thickening over the tracks and creeping towards—and asks, "So, what was it we're going to City Hall about? The train outages? Your Robocop conspiracy?"

June picks up her pace along with her response, "I want to show you what they did about her children, poor babies."

Kipling doesn't quite understand June's phrasing, but doesn't dwell on it.

She goes on, "The moth laid a bunch of eggs on the sidewalks at the bases of buildings. And up on the buildings, some specific buildings it turns out."

Kipling gets the sense she's enjoying her own dramatization. It helps him to ignore his own incredulity.

"I don't know what anyone tried to do about them, but it wasn't long before they hatched. The adult didn't eat, just looked around for the right spot, and . . . So, they thrive on, what? Leaves, wood you think? Central Park?

Naw, it's not plants. It's too weird. Calcium. Limestone. The caterpillars were eating the sidewalks and buildings; then, they started spinning their webs. Everything escalated from there. Escalated way the fuck up there. I got a bone to pick with City Hall, yeah, see, but, well I was kinda jokin.'"

Kipling hears a sweetness this time. The mania and anger she keeps putting on keeps slipping off. Every story just gets sadder. The righteous fire and brimstone she keeps alluding to—it rises for a moment, but quickly extinguishes.

He shakes his head to himself, denying that it makes any sense. Is he inserting his own—moth—feelings into her words? Is she really, earnestly opening up, and is he missing it, lost in this anxiety dream?

"Besides all that," June says, "I thought you were just living the 'Big Lie' like everyone else, but I see you're really fucked in a different way. It's OK, at least it's authentic. Almost, uh, well . . . I like you, see? You remind me of some anime protagonist who thinks that every time he faces off against the monster it's the first time. Or, is that like *Memento*? Are you like *Memento*?"

"Am I?" Kipling's hoarse. He's been breathing this dusty subterranean air for a while now, and they haven't had anything to drink.

"Well, whatever you are, we gotta switch lines again."

Well-lit mosaics on more white-tiled walls come into view up ahead, indicating another station. As they get closer the mosaics become readable. <MONEY> and

<LUCK> set in Traditional Chinese writing flanks CANAL ST., written in English. The extended platform leads into a station with working lights. June wastes no time towing Kipling up the nearest stairs off of the platform and into the pedestrian underpass between the yellow line's platforms and the green's. Though completely abandoned, these passages are almost spotless, leaving Kipling in further doubt about the reality of any bit of the current situation.

They're back on the Lexington line—the green, the '5' as it would have been traveling. The labyrinth of silken tapestries they had left behind is no longer behind them. Luckily June doesn't subject them to trying to navigate through the webs. Kipling thinks he catches a fascination in her expression as she looks down the tunnels.

Departing the station, he notices something about their footsteps, too. Is there an echo? No. Was there before?

They stay on the extended platform, close to the wall, walking without talking for another good stretch before June slows down and turns to Kipling. "My phone battery is getting low, can we use yours for now? You go on ahead. We'll get to Brooklyn Bridge Station any minute now, but we'll just go straight through, sticking to the right wall when it curves. You'll see. There's an old, unused spur of track that hooks off the main lines there."

The oppressive lack of reverb bothers Kipling even more in this position. He turns on his phone light and shines it only a few feet ahead, afraid to waiver. Afraid to look at anything that he doesn't believe should be there. He even worries that June will admonish him about wasting his time, looking at nothing. This isn't June in his head, of course, and he knows it. But, it doesn't stop him from protecting his psyche—acting as if it's true.

The tunnel widens gradually as they get to the station. Kipling hears the scurrying of some kind of commuters from out in the darkness to his left.

June skips forward up next to him as the platform widens to allow it. "Thanks, you're doing great." She whispers cheerily into his ear before slipping back into single-file behind him.

He accepts the affirmation with suspicion. He briefly wonders why she's trying to stay behind him here. He carries on, however, and the platform narrows again. Not long after which the tunnel curves away into a tiny tributary—the right wall when it curves.

This smaller subway tunnel seems clear of any webs, maybe even less dusty than the larger tunnels they've trod through so-far. Patterned brickwork and glazed mosaic tile decorate vault arches in a style more distinct than even the artifacts back at 14th.

This line's curve hooks left while they continue along its right wall. A light around the bend shines harshly. The air is different here—there's movement to it and very little dust. Even the shadows seem sharper. Kipling notices the rails below—dull and orange—the ties split and dried from a century of weather and disuse.

They reach the light where the tunnel opens, and both stop to gape.

The City Hall station platform opens in a wide stroke. Daylight streams through metalwork skylights set into the vaulted ceiling. Glass once set in leaded frames. Now the frame is all that's left, letting unfiltered light shine in from above. Late morning's sunrays catch on the intricate Guastavino tilework covering the arches—highlighting patterns of pearl, jade, and mahogany in ornate stripes and zigzags. Brass chandeliers hang suspended, tarnished and warped.

"Beautiful, right?" June says, her voice soft with reverence. "Like they actually gave a damn when they built it." She runs her hand along the wall, feeling the contrast of texture and temperature. Rough brickwork at platform level, smooth tiles when she reaches up to touch the vaults.

Kipling nods wordlessly, forgetting his aches and confusion, absorbing the elegance of the space. The skylights cast perfect columns of light through the air, dust motes dancing in the beams.

"Never knew this was here," he finally manages.

"Most don't anymore. Station's been closed to trains since the nineteen-forties. Safety standards changed, and maintenance was never pushed for." June looks up to an arch bearing the text CITY HALL. There's a staircase beneath it. "They used to run tours here, before everything else happened."

She walks up the stairs, her footsteps echoing in the cavernous space. Kipling follows, his eyes drawn to the Romanesque arches and the delicate mosaic work that somehow survived decades of neglect. Unlike the tunnels they'd been walking through, there's a pristine quality here—as if this space exists outside of time. The only obvious disturbances of season, directly below the open skylights.

"Why'd you bring me here?" Kipling asks, and qualifies, "I don't buy everything you're saying, but I'm really curious about the trains, and—" He cuts off without admitting that he wants to let her get to her point before putting her down.

June pauses on the stone landing. "Oh? I wanted you to see something beautiful before we go up."

"'beautiful before' . . . Go up where?"

"City Hall Park."

Some patience cracks within him, "That's it? We walked all this way to see a park?" Kipling tries to sound dismissive, but there's a tremor in his voice he can't quite control. Hiking through subway tunnels for an hour or three to see a park he could have reached in fifteen minutes by cab suddenly seems like the most useless way to spend the morning—especially considering his obvious pain and continuing stress.

June studies him, "No. We walked all this way so you could see what no one wants to admit."

Before he can ask what she means, she starts up the next staircase. Kipling hesitates, then follows, trying to ignore the growing ache in his feet on top of the reopened cut on his shin dripping onto the smooth steps.

The stairs lead to a mezzanine level above the platform. At the center of this space is a different kind of skylight—a circular oculus that sends a perfect round spotlight onto the worn floor below. Wire conduits and pipes have been installed along the walls, modern intrusions on the historical space.

Their pace has slowed to a few steps at a time while June watches Kipling take it all in.

"You still with me?" June asks as they approach another, steeper staircase beyond the mezzanine. "These go straight up to the park. When we get out, City Hall will be right behind us. Everything else to see will be right in front of us." She smiles stating the facts.

They climb the steeper stairs. At the top is a metal, verdigris hutch, sunlight streaming through its windows. June takes the stairs two at a time, rocketing out of the subway before Kipling has a chance to object.

He hesitates at the bottom of the stairs. Something about the light flooding down feels wrong—too bright, too direct. His heart pounds in his chest as he forces himself up the steps, his thoughts unable to stick to the here and now. How long did this walk take? It couldn't have been more than a couple hours. Is it afternoon already? Did he see someone he knew at the building this morning? What happened to the trains? Where was he going when he came down here?

His mind is still chasing the past while his body begrudges the present. Kipling emerges into harsh sunlight, squinting as his eyes adjust. The hutch opens onto what used to be a path in City Hall Park. In front of them, a concrete fountain stands proudly with a rococo golden spire on an imperial orb. However, the fountain stands dry, and the park around it stands bare.

Where trees stood tall and verdant in the summer, now burnt sticks hunch splintered. What were cultivated gardens, now rogue saplings and wild grasses. Possibly, the most striking contrast of all—and, at-first, truly unnoticed by Kipling—is the missing parallax of concrete towers. The background of metropolis, the Financial District itself, decimated. Though, beyond the old subway entrance behind them, City Hall seems mostly intact. Looking west they can almost see Jersey City poking over the horizon. The view, no longer obstructed by quite as much architecture.

Only the bones and cracked flesh of the buildings remain on this part of the island. The scene, an indelible memorial to an unspoken Armageddon. Strands of silk stream in the breeze—banners waving on broken spears. What concrete structures remain, scored with carbon black streaks and spots suggesting grim faces on funerary monuments. Rebar pierces out cruciform over Golgothan piles. Glass itself is completely absent from any remaining steel hashwork. It's all been crushed, burned, and precipitated down to the ground. Mounds of glass, silk, rocks, and mud range across the streets, burying most of the asphalt under minor landfills.

As his eyes adjust to the bright sunlight, Kipling is almost able to process what he's seeing. He looks around, frowning slightly.

"Huh," he says, with understated confusion, "Park seems bigger than I remember."

June gives him a sidelong glance before some other idea comes to mind and she steps up close to him.

Kipling doesn't know what to focus on, the sudden waft of B.O. and his own vomit coming off of June, what his nose is trying to distract his eyes from seeing, or rather . . . the sky . . . ?

June catches him before he hits the ground.

Kipling opens his eyes, waking up to a barely audible ambient tone. A hum below tinnitus, like being on the inside of an unrung bell. The sound of the space starts to remind him of his body. His parched throat, killing him with every breath. His shin, sore. His shoulder and hip, also strangely sore. He has been lying on a thin, coarse rug that doesn't really protect him from the cold marble floor underneath it. His skin is frigid to his own touch.

Pushing his aches to stand up, he tries to generate some spit and fails, wincing at another breath. The floor, as he noticed, is marble, the walls are marble, the stairs—which rise a few steps in front of him and then split up in two, into a curl around the room—also marble. The railings may even be ivory here, they're so white he's reluctant to touch them. His hands are caked with dirt, glitter, probably still some vomit.

Directly above, rectangular windows in a Georgian rotunda are letting in a little bit of indirect light. A coffered dome caps the room, held up by Corinthian pillars. A lofted wrap-around floor can be reached by the twin staircases. Kipling feels reborn in this secure, substantive temple. Waking here devoid of context, his delusion clears—or twists. A profane interloper in a serene secular cathedral, he surrenders to a sense of sacred enchantment.

Kipling grabs hold of the banister and starts to ascend the left flank of stairs. Every successive grasp to steady himself leaves behind more reeking traces of grime. The clops of his footsteps persist between every moment, dominating the ambience as he climbs. At the top landing, where both serpentine staircases remeet, he stops and grips the pulpit-shaped handrail with both hands. Relieved to refrain from further desecration. Something is tugging at his attention. A doubt, or presence.

He turns around, looking along the rounded half-floor—reminded of the elegant, looping train station below. He looks at his hands again. He looks at his torn, dirty pants. He remembers the moth. He remembers June. He looks up and sees her across the rotunda, on the same level opposite this landing. She frowns and shakes her head, then holds up her hand. He takes that to mean he should wait right here.

June approaches cautiously, uncertain of Kipling's state.

Still half-way across the round she says, "We both need showers."

Kipling doesn't know how to reply. Almost can't reply with how dry he feels.

"You've been lying to me, to yourself. Like all the rest of them. You're just better at it." June's pace slows as she speaks. "Or worse at it, maybe. Whichever it is, I still want to make it easier for you."

In this hall, with the pillars behind him, Kipling feels a growing awareness. Inner presence. In the correct place. The lights shining at his back. He can let go of his armor of ignorance.

When she gets near to Kipling, he's still facing out over the railing, his back to her. He feels a chilled breeze on his face through the broken windows of the tower.

June steps forward. Her hand gently finds his back and Kipling lets go of the railing, turning to face her. Finding a way to rasp through his desiccated larynx, he whispers, "Is it real, the moth?"

June reaches out to grip both of his shoulders and look him in the eyes, searching and kind, "It is."

"Can we do anything about it?"

"Maybe from here we can."

VII

For Sale: A House in Snatches

~ Elou Carroll

The house does not disappear all at once. Neither does it reappear in the same manner. Instead, Shannon rolls her shoulders, sighs and glowers up at discombobulated portions, at a house deconstructed: a sconce here, attached to nothing but empty air; half a kitchen, complete with electric lights still shining and the scent of baking in its partial oven; an old woman, a previous owner perhaps, rocking in the back bedroom—if the back bedroom were two thin planks attached to a sliver of grimly-painted wall.

The old woman eyes Shannon as she hammers the seventh consecutive *For Sale* sign into the sometimes-present garden, at one moment surrounded by a tangle of wild flowers and the next bordered only by mole-humped mounds of disturbed earth. Shannon stares back.

"Come on, you old bat," she calls up to her. Shannon is familiar with the stubbornness of houses—and the ones who linger in them. Shannon is an expert in difficult buildings, and she's not going to let this run roughshod over her career. "You have to give it up sometime."

Then, the back bedroom is no longer.

Now, there is a sitting room, complete right down to the plush patterned carpet and a small boy with a wooden train. Shannon's hand clenches on the mallet-handle: this is new.

Usually, a house will reveal itself quickly, take stock of her and scream until she goes away, or until it loses its large voice and finds her still standing in front of it, mallet in hand, sign in ground. Shannon has been with this house for weeks—her signs disappearing and reappearing in segments just as the house does—and she has never seen the boy.

Before the estate agent can decide whether she wants to introduce herself, call out to the boy and see if he can hear her, the train stills and the boy looks up. Shannon holds the mallet closer to her chest—his eyes are so bright, so alive that her arms bump with gooseflesh.

Shannon clears her throat and stands up straight. "Hello," she says to the boy.

He doesn't speak, not at first. Instead, he tilts his head, stands, runs the little train back and forth along the side of his thigh as if he might be thinking. The boy stares at Shannon in the way that animals stare before they bite— or before they roll over and bare their belly for a scratch. Shannon has never kept animals, but she thinks she ought to let him get a sniff of her, just in case.

She steps forward; a polite, round paving stone materializes beneath her feet and she resists the urge to say *thank you.*

The boy doesn't move.

Another step, another paving stone. Shannon has never been able to get anyone inside this particular house. No sooner does the door appear than it disappears when the suggestion of an approach stirs in her chest.

"Can you hear me?" she asks.

He considers her for a moment, and then boy and train skip across the carpet to the warped wooden door. When he leaves the room, it disappears. When he enters the hallway, it grows around him like a fungus. The door weeds up from the ground between them and the boy pulls it open. "I can hear you," he says.

She shouldn't go any closer. She knows she shouldn't go any closer. Nothing good happens when you get too close to a troublesome house, but she keeps *that* to herself. The alternative is bad for business. In truth, Shannon has never ventured inside any of the houses she's sold. All of the tours are self-guided—after signing a hefty waiver, of course—and if the potential buyers don't make it out? Well, they were warned. Shannon knows better than to enter a house like this.

And yet.

The remaining paving stones sprout in front, one by one—an inviting trail of original granite circles, dipped and scored with age. Around them the white-and-yellow pop of daisies and dandelions. A soft spray of baby's breath brushes her bare ankles, gently coaxing her forwards.

The boy smiles without showing his teeth. His cheeks puff up and Shannon cannot help but smile back at him.

She glances at her watch, she's got nowhere to be for a few hours yet and wouldn't it be brilliant if she could get a better idea of the layout? Perhaps even take photographs for the listing. Shannon chews the inside of her cheek: she's not impulsive. Shannon makes plans, right down to which socks she's going to wear every morning—a decision she makes on a Sunday evening before bed. This is risky. This is not part of the plan.

And yet.

The portion of the kitchen fades out of view and the scullery behind replaces it. The old woman is there now and she is scowling. The old woman moves tins and jars and boxes, picking them up and putting them back down with increasing ferocity. Whatever she's looking for, it's no longer there.

"So that's why you're still here . . ."

"Are you coming?" calls the boy.

Shannon's head hasn't decided but her feet are unperturbed. Her feet are walking to the door even as she frets and thinks, and by the time she makes a decision, she's already there. Her hand is already pulling the door shut behind her.

Shannon turns back half-expecting the door to be gone already, but it remains solid and shut. Through the little window, Shannon sees not the street she left, with her own over-large car parked in front, but the garden in full bloom. Past it, there are houses but not the ones Shannon recognizes. These are older, long-since bull-dozed and replaced with something more modern—a fate that would have befallen this house too, if not for the fact that it wasn't entirely there to begin with. Well, perhaps not to begin with. Shannon doesn't know the history; all she knows is that it's a hard sell, who wants a house that isn't all there?

"Shit."

Shannon tries the handle but it doesn't budge.

"Double shit."

The boy is at the end of the hallway, the train still in his hand. He watches her dither by the door, his smile unchanging.

"Well, since I'm inside . . ."

She expected it to be hazy, dreamlike, but the floor is firm beneath her feet, the walls are solid and the air is filled with the scent of age and damp and something meaty. When she moves down the hallway, Shannon glances into each room she passes, slips her phone from her pocket and snaps a photo. Some look as she would expect them to, others look older, much older. Straw-covered floors and evidence of horses, as if this part of the house might once have been a stable. It's possible, she thinks. A long, long time ago, this would have been sprawling farmland as far as the eye could see.

Shannon chuckles to herself—it would be easier to sell if it were farmland still.

Another room looks like it's been dropped into the house from the Seventies. All loud patterned wallpaper, garish colors and a mismatched carpet. The house doesn't seem to mind that it has two kitchens. In fact, Shannon suspects that the house is proud of the fact, and that it is hiding more of them between its walls. As she wanders, she sees every decade laid out with its most questionable of decorating choices.

One room in particular, however, looks like nothing she has ever seen. Sleek and featureless but with creases down the walls and the floor that suggest furniture hidden away from view. The whole thing glows a muffled white though there isn't a light source to be seen. Shannon expected a haunting, some dead old crone—the one she sees daily—tearing the house asunder and clinging onto the pieces, but this is something else entirely.

And the house is bigger, much bigger, than it should be.

"I'm going to have to up the price . . ." she mutters.

Up above, the floorboards creak and something rasps a gaping breath. *The old woman*, Shannon tells herself. *It has to be.*

She's never seen anyone else at this house but then again, she'd never seen the boy until this morning either. Perhaps there is a whole family of disjointed apparitions not-living here. More than one. Maybe there is a family for every time period, and they will all have to leave.

But it would never be so easy as simply saying *Cheerio!* and waving them off. No, they will need evicting.

Shannon does not handle evictions.

Evictions are carried out by specialists who either have a death wish or receive vast amounts of hazard pay, and Shannon has neither of those things.

What she does have are several questions regarding her life choices; at least, the ones she's made today, the most pertinent of which is: *What, exactly, were you thinking?*

She should have stayed outside, called out to the boy and spoken at a distance. The Shannon of last week wouldn't have dreamt of it, walking right up to the house and stepping in like it was ordinary, like she'd been invited for tea.

The boy does not look at the empty, formless room. If he's aware of its existence, he ignores it but Shannon had seen him run the train across the open doorway as if there was a wall there all along. He wears old clothing, the sort of clothing you might see in photos of evacuees in wartime—perhaps, she thinks, he can only see the parts of the house that match himself.

Why, then, can she see the room that time hasn't made yet? Shannon is a creature of the present, and there certainly isn't a room like that in the present.

As if to answer her question, and as if realizing for the very first time, the boy says, "You are not part of the house."

Shannon wets her lips. Houses like flattery, especially the tricky ones. "No, but I'd like to be," she says. "All the better—so that I can introduce the perfect person, people, to their perfect new home."

The boy frowns.

Shannon fishes her business card from her pocket, it's a little crumpled now. "I'm an estate agent. See? I'm like a matchmaker between people and houses."

"But we live in this house," he says.

"I think 'live' is a relative term—but who is 'we'?" It's entirely too easy and as soon as the question is out, Shannon knows she won't be getting an answer. The boy simply smiles and skips further down the corridor.

"C'mon," he calls without looking back.

A house is a hungry thing, and above all else a house likes to eat. All houses, even the ordinary ones. One might like the taste of single socks, underwear and unpaid bills, another might have a preference for the technological, television remotes and mobile phones. Many a house takes the taste of metal between its teeth, with keys and hair clips and grips and the odd spoon or two. Troublesome houses, like this one, well, they might like something a little bit more meaty.

As Shannon follows the boy up the stairs, the sensation of being swallowed rushes into her belly.

The old woman is at the top of the stairs, her scowl still fixed in place. The boy is next to her now, his free hand holding the folds of her skirt. The old woman has her arms crossed and Shannon knows that even if she asks nicely, the old woman will not move for her.

"Is this your grandmother?" she asks.

The boy nods. The old woman glances down at him but otherwise does not move.

Shannon expects her to shout, to tell her in no uncertain terms to *Get out and take that blasted sign with you*, but she doesn't. The more Shannon looks at the old woman, the more she can see the whorls of the floorboards reflected in her wrinkles, the pattern of the wallpaper on her dress.

The boy too has on him echoes of the house; the shirt that peeks out from beneath his vest holds the same pattern as the tiles that make up the kitchen floor.

Just as before there is the sound of something large, and breathing. Shannon casts a nervous glance behind and witnesses the house changing, another room appearing—the house.

Her gaze snaps back to the old woman and the boy and both of them are smiling now.

The boy is showing his teeth.

And they are sharp.

"Oops," he says and his smile widens. The pattern of the carpet has bloomed on his vest now. The old woman's belt has become the border, a strip of wallpaper that runs along the centre of the hall, covered in musty-looking greenery. When the boy steps towards her, the old woman comes with him. They walk in tandem.

No—not in tandem. They are the same thing now. The boy has nestled himself into the side of her skirts and grows out of them now like a tumor.

"You're the house." Shannon steps back.

"Yes," they say, in a voice that is not one but many, not entirely a voice at all but the sound of stairs creaking and doors slamming and the drift of a curtain in the wind. The sound, too, of shifting floorboards, of a kettle boiling on the stove, the light *ding!* of a microwave and the abrupt *pop!* of a bulb bursting. The sound of rubble moving, foundations being laid, walls being demolished. They speak like a house being made and unmade, lived in and abandoned, and all of the voices of those who've been and gone whisper along with it. Shannon can even hear her own voice in that single-word cacophony.

She steps back once more—and misses. Her heel slips from the step and Shannon falls with a sickening crunch. Her head catches the bannister and the house blooms with mould. The pristine hallway that she had walked down festers with rot and damp and Shannon is laying in it, her lower leg at a terrible angle.

The house does not hurry, the old woman and her boy descend the stairs at an agonizing pace. There is no need for them to move any faster, Shannon isn't going anywhere.

But she tries, ever so hard. Shannon rips the nails from their beds, shoving them between the crumbling floorboards, pulling her ruined body towards the door. The door that no doubt still leads to somewhere out of time, somewhere long gone. A crunch comes from somewhen outside and the house seems to gulp. All at once the crumpled *For Sale* sign comes tumbling down from the ceiling, its broken pieces and the pieces of its six fallen brothers bury her in splinters.

"Please," she whispers.

The house—the old woman and her boy—simply smiles at her. Licks its—their—lips, just a little.

That's the thing with troublesome houses, once they get a taste of you, there's nothing they can do but bite.

Bring Me the Head of Louise Michel!

~ *Basile Lebret*

Translated from: "Apportez-moi la Tête de Louise Michel!" in *Lufthunger Pulp's vol. 3: Les Feux de la Révolte*

The petroleuses' ascension had been met with the howls of the cheering crowd beneath. From the Bastille plaza, an innumerable amount of occulars consigned this event as the last stand. Eyes rendered hard by furious massacres which had lasted for days, glassy eyes for whom the issue didn't matter anymore, children's eyes who couldn't understand the half of it, women's eyes who now stood in arms, viscous eyes beneath nictitating membranes through which no man has ever seen, few and far still glinting eyes whose hope would soon stand shattered.

You are a part of the dreamers' crowd, into which cabrechins, humans, and auriphaunes joined. Against your belly, you firmly grip the jute bag the fancy man walking beside you gave you. To the front, the sickly thin woman cuts through the crowd, an abrasive knife. The ruffians spread out, split up like the hem of a wound. The woman said nothing, will never say anything. The man tries to explain that you need to get out of Paris before the repression kicks in, that he has a plan, that the Council thought of everything, that there's but little time.

Above, the afternoon sky is hidden by this layer of smoke that's your defeat. As they retreated to the East, the Communards requested the Petroleuses light colossal arsons. A strategy which chars the heavens until they are but black sheep marbled in flames.

Nobody's completely fooled. Hearsay attest Versailles brought back Giant Worms from Gascogne; they are using the beasts to drill through buildings. Barricades offer no cover from this cowardly scheme.

That's why the fancy man and the silent woman are bringing you, through the soon-to-be-dead crowd towards a cyclopean stairway which ends in darkness.

"If Versailles had accepted our conditions, we could have had a metropolitan," complains the man in front of the gaping maw. He adds: "You and Louise are gonna use those tunnels to pass beneath the Versailles forces, this package needs to leave this hellhole, you understand? And to do that, you need to follow the rail until you hit Neuilly."

He spoke slowly as if the melanin in your skin hindered your comprehension. Without answering, you smile by sheer habit; you're tired.

"Well . . ." starts the man before a bullet barges through his mandible in a sprinkle of blood.

The silent woman puts a hand on your head, forcing you to duck, and brings you towards the underground system. Children fleeing all around and unarmed creatures run towards what they feel is the only way out. You fear being trampled, but facing the stampede you conserve your balance.

A presence passes in-between your legs. Might be an auriphaune.

It never existed.

Above, the mortars crash on the Bastille Plaza. Each impact produces a faience drizzle which rains upon survivors who tried to hide in the unfinished station.

There's space down here. Stone arches on both sides of the stairway pierce through the rock and mark the railways. A large chunk of the survivors, churned by the outside world, are now taking the escape route that will help them flee the Versailles forces.

You watch them go, suddenly very aware of the protection their presence gave you. Your grip tightens around the jute; the silent woman, she tightens her grip on your shoulder. An order to take the opposite route.

"Hey, what are you both doin'?" suddenly howls a feminine voice, through loud laughter.

You and your partner turn toward the importune as one.

They are working girls. All dolled up, almost concealed. You count six or seven of them as they close the distance between you. The silent woman has already raised her firearm, her right eye almost touches the iron sight on her Chassepot rifle.

"You aren't aiming the right way," says the voice you heard first, and whose owner is a plump brunette. Nonchalant, she puts her own weapon against her shoulder, cannon upwards. Her cohort cackles. Each one armed.

"I must take this package outside Paris," you answer, showing them the jute bag, which in the shadows seemed to be now caked in some brown liquid.

A female cabrechin, all blue and black and golden scale, mouthing a cigarette asks: "And you thought 'bout going down under to do so? That's some wishful thinking, ladies."

"I've stopped being wishful when I put makeup on this morning," laughs some blond devil whose gender you can't determine. Does it even matter?

"We can help you," continues the plump one; she appears to be their leader. "I didn't think of making it through today anyway."

The herd pushes past the both of you. Your bodyguard, the silent woman, betrays her resentment through her touch.

"Be wary of egrantines," jokes the leader while her friends chuckle in the back.

Two of the prostitutes hold lanterns whose oil was mixed with cane tree wood, to fight off evil spirits, they said. Above your veiled heads, the sky now resembles rocky intestines. Your companion's spark rebounds on the damp bricks.

The faience sprinkles of the Bastille station have disappeared for the better part of two minutes, now replaced by a silence that is way more oppressive. The public ladies, they chatter and cackle from time to time.

Soon, the tunnel opens up, giving way to what your band calls a station. According to them, some metal train was supposed to come a-blaring above the rail, enabling clients "to rest and fatten." Well, t'was the Commune plan before Thiers and his blessed-ass army came to mess things up.

The hooker squad has instinctively lowered their voices. They are now walking in a line, left hand on the shoulder of the person up front, like a genuine armed force. It's the ballet of the canon, going up and down as the line of fire becomes clear, that mesmerizes you the most.

The silent woman just put her left hand on your shoulder too, the same way as the girls, but her rifle resides besides it. You dislike being a human shield.

The place in which you stumble is littered with stained windows. If the previous name was Bastille, this one's Espace Saint-Paul. Above your head, gaslight spreads a sickly, trembling brightness. Might be this sign of human presence that silenced the harpies.

The band's step makes too much noise in this liminal space as your steps scrape off the railway stones. Both harbingers of light vainly try to pierce the obscure corners of the station. This incessant sweeping wakes up and forces the rare egrantines who dreamed in the weird and dark angles, to flee. Aside from their chitinous and hairy body, nothing appears to be moving in the wetness within.

Nothing more than you and your step which the treacherous rocks appear eager to trick. For but a moment you thought you heard the staccato of a hoard of egrantines legs over the gravel. The nightmare overpowers you. Already, the silent woman's grip forces you to regain your composure and push on. Deep down you know that contrary to their voracious appearance, egrantines aren't known to attack anything bigger than a dog.

The station, which offered itself, closes behind you without revealing anything.

As you take your first step in the entrails of the City Hall, your allies suddenly raise their weapon in unison. You suddenly realize a man is standing on the stairs leading to this blinding, darkened sky. The newcomer scans your squad, surprised, before he starts to scream. Those are no sensible words coming out of his groin but the throaty rattle first heard in grottoes sanctified by humankind. The priest, you recognize his roman collar, appears to tear off something from his celestial garment and begins to run towards your position.

To your left, the weapons crackle . . .

BOOM

. . . and the man of God implodes. Literally. The detonation forces each and everyone of you to lay on the ground, on the rail. A thin rain, made of gravel and blood, hails upon your backs.

"So now we have to fight explosive clergymen, eh?" whines the leader as her friends chuckle.

The stone roof shatters and opens like some Leviathan's jaws in unnamed seas.

Through its cyclopean innards, you discern the City Hall being devoured by flames. Up there, heavens are as black as yours. A petroleuse is desperately gripping the building facade just as a bullet storm picks her. Even higher, one of her congeners is held prisoner by the brazier they started, she howls a fear you hope you'll never have to face.

But the Versailles forces are already taking hold of the newly formed hole, growling and shooting from the hip. Through the debris and the smoke, their figures, adorned with the white costume of the Penitents, appear as obscene gnomes.

The silent woman stood before all the others. Already, she shoots at the gaping maw and its faceless mob. The dolled-up women take on the rare cover offered by the station. The female cabrechin never makes it. You watch as she lays restlessly on a mattress of her own blood.

"Sylvie! I told ya I dressed up to die!" yells one of them as gunshots crush her every word.

Your guardian pushes you towards the shadows. Towards Neuilly, if it's still accessible. Behind you, the fight intensifies, bound with laughter, then gets swallowed whole by the darkness.

For two stations, all there is the echo of your steps and this wetness you've learned to picture as France. It's a cold fug that doesn't resemble your country's. Through time, it transforms your burden into an icicle. You still firmly grip the round object.

The silent woman hasn't spoken, will never speak. She at least stopped using your body as a ballistic shield. You have always been too nice and unknowingly thank her for it. The Louvre station is the most beautiful thing you've ever witnessed; with white tiles and painting reproductions all around. The decorum let you picture what the Commune had in mind, and, by extension, what Adolphe Thiers and his ignorant masses are now destroying.

Your hands upon the jute turn tender, without noticing it you've begun to cradle the package. You think about this red madness that took over for weeks and through which the hungry people feverishly thought they had every right to decide their own fate. We used to talk up there, beneath a sky that wasn't black smoke yet, we spoke and we partied! We worked but we worked better. Soon, the Council had proclaimed humans and cabrechins were born equals, and then we had forbidden night shifts.

News outlets had spread like Palenseul bees beneath the epidermis of a tired beast. And then we'd learned Marseilles had fallen.

For sure, we took arms. We wouldn't give Paris to the Fritz, he could drop dead the Iron Emperor and all his dogs in the Council of Jules. The same who wanted to sell the newborn Republic to the Prussian invaders.

We would fight tooth and nail and to the death, that's for sure!

Soon, Thiers had organized the repression and by night he'd entered Paris through the West. Hearsay, because no newspaper would dare speak, told us that his generals executed whoever they found, humans, cabrechins, almost-arachnids.

Even so, we dreamed! And it was nice for but one week to have resided at Morpheus' palace!

The silent woman suddenly orders you to stop making noise. Nothing really changed for you since you cannot see farther than one meter through the darkness. The world is black and white, full of optical avatars created by the cones of your retina trying to fight the lack of information. As a kid, this impaired eyesight terrified you.

There is pork on the rails.

You notice them through their scent. The pigs, they oink and they dig, there are at least a dozen coming through a door cut into the wall on the right. Through their hoofed feet, you notice some atrophied hands, semi-gaures' hands and you wonder how they got in such a situation.

The tall woman closes in on the wall, she left the gravel to walk on the solid root of it. Thanks to this strategy, your footsteps can no longer be heard on this sea of stones. You doubt it's useful since the beasts' noise covers every noise you might make. The animals don't appear bothered by their predicament. From time to time, they pick a stone up, chew on it for a while before letting it fall, joyless. Bored.

When a ray of light hits your guide, your heart skips a bit. You thank God your dark body wasn't the one caught in the spark.

"Who goes there?" asks a voice, audibly coming from behind a mask. Without turning towards the source, you imagine the white cones that are the apparatus of the Versailles forces.

In front of you, the silent woman raises her hands. Her back's still facing the enemy, who came from the same doors as the piglets. There are two of them, their Chassepot rifle glistens in the moist atmosphere. None of them pays attention to the pigs. Or to you.

"Isn't that a bitch?" asks the blonde one. "Bearing arms, at that!"

In less time than Louise needs to bring down her arms about an inch, the two soldiers open fire. In the pyramid of light cast by their lantern, you see roses blooming on the albino wall as the silent woman's body jolts. She's still vainly trying to turn towards her fate with her last breath. She falls.

"Communards trash," spits the blonde one.

Behind him, you notice a red presence which wasn't there earlier. You think of the pigs, of the slaughterhouses the nobles destroyed in order to build the Tuileries. You think of the Red Man and the apparition grins at you.

For it isn't a man that stands behind the young soldier, it is an entity. It has already swung what appears a cleaver in the boy's throat. The victim jerks. And you see the creature putting her fingertip on a single drop of blood, stopping the geyser and time itself. With its index, the monster draws an arcane symbol, soon the flesh of the second man is splitting up while he tries to turn around.

His skin spreads into distinct squares, whose borders soon fill with blood, a sea of pain, they begin to fly, defying all gravity.

You only witness the beginning of his flesh blooming. The man is already screaming for a certain "Nathalie!" Inside the room behind the trio, gunshots can be heard. Their detonations appear both metallic and shrill in this catacomb.

As you run as fast as you can on the growling gravel, you only hope for one thing. Putting as much distance between yourself and the demon.

Between you and the Red Man of the Tuileries.

Nothing could stop your escape. Neither the howls of the Versailles forces, or the gunshots, not even the gigantic egrantines jumping at your toes when they notice you're alone. Your feet hurt and your left big toe is bleeding profusely. Since when? You don't know it, but if faced with a barricade you'd probably prefer to crash on the swords of Thiers' army.

This thought stops you dead in your tracks. As you gulp for air, you notice a pool of daylight in front of you, right here, right in front of you. You grip the bag and what lays hidden inside as you approach.

Pale daylight coming from the sinkhole illuminates a wall made of stones and crushed bodies. It renders the tunnel unfeasible. You snort, bothered by the rotten smell stemming from the grotesque mountain. Behind you, a lone egrantine screams before the staccato of her long legs move further away.

You need out. You think of those men on whom a demon befell. You pity them, a bit. You do so because you don't yet know what's outside. Wallowing and spiky in the manner of a hissing cat.

First hint is this liquid beneath your digit as you extract yourself off the ground. The bundle seems heavier around your waist as you sluggishly bask in the daylight. What's between your every phalange, what's spread across your garment, the street and every wall, every window, is Communards' blood.

Taken aback, you try to clean up as you stand. Buzz flies prowl on bodies all around as if they were but waste. Dead eyes, torn flesh, red and blue blood mix in the mud. You can't help but think this was all in vain.

Away, bouncing off the bullet-filled walls, bouncing off the skybox which is turning white since arsons are over, bouncing off the rare tiles still in place, bouncing off the cornet of dead ears who'll never hear again, away sounds the masquerade of gunshots. So far away, you think you dreamed it. You grip the jute bag like a kid, beneath your hand, the texture now appears gross.

But then a scream, gun fires, there, close. You crash against the first door you see. In the street, guilt and dead bodies appear inclined to let you go.

The open court shines so bright, you squint. Beyond the gate, in the street, a man is pleading not to get shot on detritus.

You stay childishly astonished by the colossal aperture in which you've made your way. Both to your left and right, an oval cut of immense dimension has been bitten through the thick inner walls.

You tremble as you think of Giant Worms from Gascogne. Seems like the Nation's Undertaker has done everything he could to regain Paris. You need only close your eyes, while a child lets out a moan, to imagine the priests and the grunts, in their white sheets, walking in line behind the bistre butt of the immense beast.

Coming from the fallen stairwell to your right, you hear a hoard of footsteps. You prepare your exit but a voice calls for you. A mother and her two kids stand up there, they seem vulgar to you, like mangled birds in some torn off cage.

"Do . . . do you have anything to eat?" she sheepishly asks.

You will not answer, passing the burden from your front to your back before entering the intestine chewed by the Giant Worms. Behind you, a small boy calls out:

"Take care, Missus!"

Then nothing.

Through the windows covered in ash and blood, shit and splintered woods, one can witness the Versailles forces executing men against the ground. Said ceremonial only exists for male humans. This you noticed although you were using all your energy to stay out of sight.

Women and cabrechins get the gun. Sometimes they're beaten across the face with the firearm cross so as not to waste a bullet. The headless dogs, abominations created in labs by Badinguet, cross the streets again and again. Whether they howl, or just stay too long in front of someone and they're done for.

You reminisce of the whispers on the Bastille Plaza. A bruise on the shoulder and you're gone, powder on your sleeves, you're gone. You don't really get how the Versailles forces operate but their decision making seems arbitrary as you slither away.

Cries which disappear in gun fires are slowly getting to you. Numerous times, you wonder what you would do if some Versailles soldier ended up begging you for his life. Would you see past the enemy? The man's history, his friends, his family?

You think of the men and women and creatures all locked up and trembling in the floors up above. Those who are on the other side of Paris, fleeing while shooting at the invading forces. The ones who said, no, we won't surrender.

Sometimes you meet an inhabitant. Rich families, tired working men, children with bloodshot eyes. For over five minutes, you wonder about entering a courtyard because some sheathing noise is coming from it. When you finally peer, it's only a blacksmith fixing some cart wheel. He stares at you with disgust, hatred and contempt lay in his watery eyes, but you also witness the fatigue that only sprouts from the bloodshed. Replete, the man continues his work and leaves you be.

If it wasn't for the thousand-yard stare and the gun shots all around, nothing seems to have happened.

The man is kneeling on the naked earth, the earth that was covered by blackened tiles, tiles who turned useless barricades. The man snorts and cries and drools in his hirsute beard. He's repeating the name of the cabochin the Versailles forces just killed.

Next to him, the headless dog growls through his naked esophagus. A mucous hoot like the one made by a hose as it turns through the air. The beast grotesquely jumps as if it could bite, but its lack of any maw prevents such an activity. A nonchalant soldier holds the creature's leash while another redneck pushes their victim's forehead towards the ground.

BLAM!

Laughter. The man on the ground is recouping his breath since the grunt shot right next to his right ear. You jumped, shocked by the indecent attitude of the executioners. You look at the bearded man's body, at the corpses all around as grotesque foundations. Women and non-human on one side, male corpses on the other. Brick and mortar torn off by bullets. Blood. The beheaded beast which screams bewildered at the mere sight of you.

His master aims and fires and the bullet pierces the window to your left, disappears. You are already running . . .

"Hey, black bitch!" yells somebody, somewhere.

. . . first through the giant aperture, then with sheer despair you push the first gate that will take you farther from the street. You feel the rush of the flying ammunition upon your neck as the soldiers miss their target. You. Wood splinters befall your tattered collar.

You pass the door, the kitchen you entered is neatly arranged, the old man drinking his coffee raises plate-sized eyes upon your pretty face. Ushering no words, you aim for another door, through its windows you distinguish a courtyard.

No time to assess, to your left must be the gate leading outside and the Versailles forces. In front of you, some austere and gray building hides dirty rooms and empty stairs. Smells like blue collar round here.

"Where's she, old man?!" yells someone behind you. The following gunshot appears too close to have permitted any answer.

From the upper floors cascade children's voices.

"Right here, right here," they squeak.

You look at them and feel pity for their frail frames. The three kids point to a corner of the courtyard with childish stubbornness. Some oval opening—a well?—covered by a grate. You don't think and with three steps, you close in on it.

Your fingers, the pain in your fingers as you grip the lumpy metal. You pull once, and some sand dislodge and rains upon the ground. You are now pulling with all your might. The harrow knocks the ground too loudly by your feet.

As you re-enter the entrails of the Earth, you don't know whether the friction you hear comes from your garment or the grunts' uniforms. Despite the cutting rocks, the blood you lay everywhere and the hematoma sprouting upon your arms, you never stop pushing forward through the cavern, through the darkness.

One of the idiots up there might fire a blind shot.

And then, you'd be done.

Experiencing total absence of light is somewhat supernatural.

You instantly realize this. It's your heartbeat reminding you of this as you use both your hands on your sandy invisible surroundings. You see nothing. You have no light source.

In pure darkness, every sound takes on extravagant explanation. No gunshot has come to your ear, and in such a sterile environment, deflagration would go a long way from your entry point to your attentive ears.

Kneeling on the moving ground, you try to recoup your breath. Every blow from the wind makes you shiver. You picture the rocks all around. Your inability to find the way you entered suddenly slaps you. Master your terror. Here, both your knees firmly stuck in the ground. Breathe. Your burden seems heavier, here, and a small creature—whatever it was—slithers upon your calves. Disappears.

When one can't turn back, all there is to do is push forward.

The stones all around take on a greenish hue. You've been walking for hours, eons, certain that will be where your journey ends. Your life.

Through your panic, you do not immediately notice you now discern your surroundings. Nothing to see really. Rocks and sharp turns dark enough to lose experienced smugglers.

You whisper to yourself that two minutes earlier you could not see a thing. So you push on towards the light, be it bioluminescent or adversary.

The place you stepped in is steeped with fungus drooling a sickly greenish light. Seated upon the ground are five terrified children. The thinner of them all raises his Chassepot rifle and vaguely aims at you. Weapon might be heavier'n he is.

"Versailles?" asks the boy with the insurance of being on the right side of the cannon.

"No, no," you stutter. You realize your throat hurts. "The Council asked me to get out of Paris."

You mentioning the Council makes them uneasy.

"Council's dead, there's no Council anymore," complains one of them.

"I know," you say although you have no idea, really. "But still, I have to get this out," you continue while presenting your burden. In the mushroom opaque light, the jute bag appears to have changed colors.

"What's inside?" requests a kid.

"Dunno."

"And you hope to make it out alive? There's worse things than Versailles down here."

"They say there are egrantines as big as big dogs!"

"Even worst!"

The virgin laid down his weapon, you thank him with a stare he might never see.

"You really think you might make it? Even though you don't know what you're carrying?"

The kid council looks at you intently.

"What else can I do?" you ask.

"You'll need a weapon then," asserts the leader while handing you their only rifle.

You know it's a trap. A bruise on the shoulder and you're gone. Powder on the sleeves . . .

"Are there really monsters down there?"

"You haven't met 'em?"

"No," you answer while picking up the loaded gun. You strap it on your shoulder like you did with your package.

On the dirt floor, one of the girls throws a nasty look to her chief.

"Which way's the exit?"

"Through here," answers the same kid while showing an opening behind him. "It's dangerous, though."

"I didn't escape the Thiers to get ate."

"Still, I wouldn't have done it."

It's the little girl who answered as you disappeared in the greenish darkness. Subconsciously, you tear one of the mushrooms from the wall. Have you ever had the choice?

The blight green radiance from the mushroom keeps the sickly pale crabs at bay. You don't really know what they are but the heavy weight of the Chassepot upon your back now reassures you. Egrantines, pseudocrabs, whatever these tunnels desire offering, you are certain you could fight it.

Despite the glow, it's your hands that first notice the change in your environment. Five minutes later, the darkness all around started to smell like rotten eggs. You felt secure in not using a regular torch and then the odor went away. You pondered about its disappearance, know now that you just got used to it.

Beneath your digits, you feel the chitin that breathes. Its plastic rigor, its life, the naked flesh which trembles beneath like some underground torrent. You already took off the wall which is really a patchwork of legs. You distinguish precisely every joint the body parts possess. You thank God, heavens, whatever deity not to have seen their bodies. Not yet.

It looks like a banana hand. You think it brownish despite the mushroom poisonous brightness turning everything lake placid green. All the legs bound into the mural sometimes shiver as if taken by a spam. You would not put your hand upon it ever again. For you fear you'll wake up the hoard it's made of.

Problem is this gross plug stands behind you and the only exit. You've been walking for more than two hours without ever noticing another opening, no crossroad. No issue.

Since you need to get out, you bend. The insectoid hand does not touch the ground, instead it hovers like vivid stalactites. Looking at it from beneath, one notices the non-existing wind which still appears to make the legs move. Like a drowned woman's hair in the current.

A shiver bites your back at the mere sight of the pod. You first try to reason, then you bargain. You need to pass beneath this. The kids told you it was the only way.

The dirt and the droppings fulfill your corset, you sneer. You think yourself ridiculous when you think of all those spiky legs right above your back, awaiting the bite like great sharks in black oceans, you want to turn back.

But there exist Thiers' rifles and the moors made of blood and the woman whose entrails were pried open like jewelry boxes. For but an instant, you picture yourself lying on your back, eyes unmoving as the dirty gray sky of the Capital weighs down upon your pupils. There's blood in the corner of your mouth and none of your eyes close when a raindrop scorches them.

You jerk your head and one of your braids hits one of the appendages. The leg extends, cracking disgustingly, it stabs the ground three times before it shivers like a manic addict, finally gets back up.

You don't dare move; you don't dare breathe. You breathe in slowly. Vast gulps of air, as wide and dense as the sky over charred bodies.

You begin to crawl anew.

With the mushroom between your teeth, the vicious legs for sole heavens as they touch your hair, you desire death. Because everything is for too long. Because you're scared. Every time you close your eyes in order to breathe, you picture the slithering skies like the voracious tails of mermaids.

You don't know it but you're crying, and the sand you carry with every push forward is slowly turning into a brick wall in front of you. One hand before the other. Right arm, left arm. Head stuck to the ground, barfing on what is certainly dried guano.

Could be worse. The arthropod banana could awake.

You don't want to picture the innards of it. Even less since it's so vast. You feel like you've crossed the desert. Reminds you of your escaping Georgia. You might have to crawl for five meters, might be one, when one of the legs stabs the sand right past your eyes.

The appendage is so close it's blurry. You picture the creatures touching your nose, you picture yourself standing up. Feeling the pressure of all those legs as the colony notices, understands, swallows you.

You feel hot and cold around your throat. The leg isn't there. With its innumerable joints that turned it tentacle.

Past your back, you still feel the weight of the million legs through which you dreamed to crashed.

☉

You try to tidy up once you extract yourself from the bowel. Like those girls who studied and were raised in good families. You take the mushroom out of your mouth; it shines a little less now that it's covered in droppings. You spit. Obviously.

The creatures that now surround you are much bigger than the pens you just left. They sleep, snoring in the blackest corners in the manner of sunken ships. You don't have the words for it, but if you were to survive and your grandson asked about it, you would answer they had legs and their maws were hard to discern. Maybe their bodies were nothing more than one starving mouth.

You gulp and the taste reminds you you've been eating shit for the last ten minutes. A whole lifetime. There is no doubt that it's the obscurity that protects your mind from shattering the insanity which swallows humans when faced with arachnids. From its sheath, you're certain one of them is bound to barge.

Your steps, your steps are so silent on the ground made of shit and dirt that no noise bounces off the walls. You suddenly notice how loud your breathing really is but this doesn't seem to have bothered the beasts. You close your eyes, count to ten and push on. Without ever turning back towards the hand that isn't really made of bananas, nor the abominations which snore in the ornate alcoves. Not even when one of them starts to rattle their teeth.

For over thirty seconds, long enough that you think the colony might chase you.

Nothing happened.

You'll forever remember the shatter of the teeth of those that lay beneath Paris. You realize this as you enter the golden glow of the sun. What you thought a cavern, then a dismantled church, are but a few walls and a fallen roof. Its features hard to discern through the desolation.

The edifice, probably a laundry, enabled the inhabitants to access the source you're walking through in order to leave the suburbs.

Above your head, a pink-blue sky melts the purple of the dying night. The bag weighs hard upon your arching neck. You fall to the ground before you throw away the shitty mushroom and wash your hands.

You inhale deeply, pushing away the events from last night. You don't doubt that through your journey, Thiers crushed every ounce of the rebellion out of the Commune's body. You still smile as you sink your hand inside the bag.

You first touch what seems like hair before you feel something viscous and so you take your hand out. You sit, and with prudence, extract a female head out of the jute. You instantly recognize the emaciated face, the somber and closed eyes. You take the blood caked letter.

The missive claims your mission does not end here. On the other side of the ocean, an immigrant named Tesla built a machine which reads deceased minds. Inside of Louise Michel's head, the Paris council recorded their every thought and last wish. Always the martyr, she turned her mind experimental palimpsest.

You're hopeless so you scream. The rage of making it. The rage of losing it all.

But then you get up.

For you still have an ocean to cross.

Séance at the Jukebox

~ Brian U. Garrison

Like a fortune teller channeling
your dead aunt, the jukebox
is just a medium. Musicians
decompose, sending ghostly chills
with every inspiration and exhalation.
A message from beyond is not atonement,

but it's the closest you can get for 25¢.
And so the coins flow—as above,
so below—falling, caught, collected—
spinning never-ending revolutions.
Dancers possessed by lyrical revelations
mimic the music with shapeless excitations.

And the dance floor would be devilish
if shaped like a scaled-down replica
of the rippling Adirondack mountains,
but it is exactly that morphing movement
of spikes and valleys—the warped air molecules
—that keeps your heart pumping to the beat.

V

Jesus Christ and Snow White

~ *H. L. Fullerton*

You sit beside the bed and hold his hand. It is limp in yours, yet warm. You feel the life trapped inside. Machines beep rhythmically, an almost comforting sound. You squeeze his hand and imagine his fingers curl around yours, just once more, please God, once more. It'd be easier to pretend if not for the smells. No matter how nice the place, underneath the antiseptic is the smell of shit and urine, of sour sweat and fetid breath, of waiting death. You block it out, swallow back the tears. You say, in a whisper, "Open your eyes. Blink, dammit, please." But your sleeping beauty doesn't.

His parents, they never liked you. They were polite but disapproving. You didn't see them often, every other Thanksgiving, but now they're here all the time. You hate the sound of their weeping. It is acid rain on your flimsy hope. You wish they'd leave and never come back. They beg you with their eyes, let him go, let him rest. You ignore their exasperated *Henrys*. You hold power of attorney; you are his health care proxy. You push aside the thought that you also have his DNR, which you've hidden away. Your love didn't want extraordinary measures taken to keep him alive, but you're not ready for him to die. You don't want to be left alone.

You are holding out for a miracle. You tell yourself, *They happen every day.*

Doctors and nurses come and go, exchanging knowing glances over your head. They speak in low, kind voices, telling you he won't wake up, the machines are all that keep him alive. They suggest you prepare yourself, that you say your goodbyes. You never make eye contact with them. You can't let yourself see the truth in theirs. You can't let anyone see the crazy in you. Instead you say, "I think he moved his index finger, just the first joint. That's a good sign, yes?"

Their voices drip with pity. They remind you it is unlikely given the severe brain damage. They scribble on his chart and promise to run tests, but you know they won't. They have run all their tests which all said the same thing, but you stopped listening long ago. You tell yourself, *Science doesn't know everything.*

Weeks go by and your conviction flutters into despair. You almost say, *Okay, pull the plug.* But you have an idea. You know a man, or of him. You worked in a nursing home in college, mopping floors, covering the stench with disinfectant. There was a woman, Arvede. First day on the job, a young Haitian named Lucien pointed her out and said, "You want to keep this job, don't cross Arvede." She'd worked there forever, knew everything about everyone. She pronounced your name in the French way, Onree. "Onree," she'd say, "you a good boy. You go work the third floor, Arvede will clean the basement." After a few months, you figured out Arvede only worked the basement when the morgue was occupied. Someone told you her cousin owned a funeral home. You believed that until one night, you met the cousin. Then you understood why some of the staff crossed themselves when Arvede walked by.

You caught a glimpse of a man striding up to the loading dock as you were taking the trash out. His skin was dark, too dark to make out facial features in the dim, yellow light cascading over the dock. It turned his cream linen suit and matching fedora the color of stale piss. He had a walking stick, but no limp. He bounded up the steps and into the building. He didn't spare you a glance. Curious, you hurried to the dumpster, lobbed in the bags and jogged back. You checked out the cars in the parking lot. A gray Cadillac was the only one that seemed out of place. There wasn't any hearse. You told yourself, *Doesn't mean anything. He could be a visitor.*

You didn't see him in the halls, but hung around where you could watch the entrance to the morgue. You'd cleaned in there a few times. It wasn't anything special, just a small room to store bodies wrapped in sheets until the funeral home picked them up. Generally, there weren't more than two corpses at a time. This was a small, expensive, private home. They made their money by keeping people alive for as long as possible.

You got paged and had to mop up vomit in the cafeteria. You worried he'd leave before you returned. You thought about asking Arvede if the man you couldn't quite see was her cousin and wondered if that would offend her. But you didn't have to. As you came around the corner, you caught sight of him exiting the morgue, ebony walking stick in hand. His skin as dark as the cane. But his face . . . three slashes on the cheek you could see, as if long ago someone had clawed him. You wondered who had marked him and, as if your thought announced your presence, he turned his head toward you. You saw the matching scars on the other cheek. He smiled at you, wide and welcoming. You broke out in a sweat. Arvede exited the morgue behind him, leading a young man, but your eyes were locked on the smiling man in the linen suit. Arvede saw you and said, "Onree, this is my cousin Uti." She looked at her cousin and said in a deeper, almost warning tone, "Onree is a good boy."

Uti broke the gaze between you and said to her, "I hope so." Then, ignoring you, he took the arm of the second man from Arvede and they made their way to the exit. As Arvede watched you watching them, you realized you knew the other man. He was Tyler Klein from 204. The twenty-something coma boy who passed away unexpectedly this afternoon. You said to Arvede, "Uti is the cousin with the funeral home?" And she said, "That's right." And you knew that gray Cadillac belonged to the man with the scarred face and you knew why he didn't bring a hearse. He walked the dead out.

You think about this as you hold your love's hand.

⊙

You drive over the bridge, watch the sun twinkle across the water. Your knuckles whiten. You didn't consider this part, seeing that wide expanse of water, feeling the gentle sway of the bridge. A horn blares and you jump, your foot hitting the accelerator. Memory creeps in. You weren't there when the accident happened, but have imagined it so many times. A bridge, a truck, a river. Water rushing in, drowning the car, filling his lungs. A sob escapes you. Then you are on dry land once more and the despair falls away. Purpose fills you: find Arvede, find the cousin. You have no plan, only this scrambling need clawing at your insides, tearing you to pieces.

You arrive at your old place of employment. You don't know where else to start. Maybe she still works here, maybe HR will have an address. You park and stare at the building. You've parked by the loading dock, as if you expect her to be waiting for you in the morgue. You think, *This is crazy.* Then get out and walk inside. You find an elevator and press the button. You wait.

You see a short, stocky man wearing a badge and a ring of keys. His shirt is the same faded green color you wore when you worked here. The elevator opens and, instead of getting in, you call out to him. He sees your crumpled clothes and assumes you are lost; tries to get you to take the elevator to the first floor. You say, "Facilities? Is it still on this floor?"

He says, "I can clean. What room?"

You explain you are looking for the office. You tell him you used to clean here. "Arvede?" you ask, but he doesn't recognize that name. He gestures in the direction of the office and you follow the halls until you find it. It has moved since your day. You stand outside the door and think, *What now?*

You open the door and go in. A secretary is on the phone. Something's leaking on the fourth floor. She promises to send someone, hangs up and gives you a strange look. She probably doesn't get many walk-ins. You search your memory for the name of your old supervisor. You picture him clearly: beer belly, thinning hair, crooked teeth. Jesus, he's probably dead by now. Jerry, John, Joe. It began with a J. Joe sounds right. You go with that. You explain you used to work here. You ask if Joe is in. "No," the woman says. "He's been gone seven, eight years. Lucien's in charge," she says. "Do you want to speak with him?"

Yes, you do. Your palms tingle. Joe would've been little help, maybe he would have given you Arvede's address, maybe not. He'd been a bastard. But Lucien . . . You tell yourself, *This is fate.*

Lucien recognizes you right off. "Henry?" he says. "My god, it's you. What are you doing here?" He invites you into his cramped office, says, "You don't look so good. You need your old job back?"

"Arvede still here?" You try to make it a casual request, but he sees through you.

He shakes his head. "Henry, man, you don't want to go there. Things can't be bad as that."

You press him and he says she's been gone a long time, has no idea where, maybe started her own cleaning company. You almost ask about the cousin, does he know where Uti is? But if he's this reluctant to tell you about her, he'll never tell you about him. "Lucien," you say, "I really need to speak with Arvede. Please tell me where I can find her."

"The Dupres are bad business," he says. "It's better if you don't find them. Men who go to the Dupres don't always return." He stares at you with heavy eyes and you back down. You thank him. Tell him he's right. You won't go looking for Arvede. You pretend you're glad he talked sense into you. You get back into your car and think, *Dupre.*

You go to a nearby library and charm the clerk into letting you use the computer even though you don't have a card. You search for funeral homes and people with the last name Dupre. There are dozens, but no Arvede or Uti. You are not deterred. You call each name, every home. You leave messages, identifying yourself as Onree. You pray she remembers the name of the skinny college boy who mopped floors fifteen years ago. You say, "Please call." Days go by. No one does.

You can't think about anything else. You squeeze your love's hand and whisper, *Hold on.*

☉

You brave the bridge a second time. You'll beg Lucien this time, threaten if you have to. He can't keep this information from you. You *need* it.

But you never make it to Lucien's office. An angel catches your eye. Your heartbeat quickens. A cemetery. You turn in. You creep along the narrow road, eyes scanning the rows of graves. The dead have been here all along and you never noticed. You wonder how many of the coffins lie empty.

You spot two workers, sitting on graves, smoking in the summer's heat. You stop the car and walk towards them. They don't stand, but wait for you to get close. One of the men says, "Office back that way." He points in the direction you came from. You put your hands in your pockets to keep from shivering. Your body thinks its winter. You ignore the coolness licking your bones. You say, "I'm looking for Arvede Dupre."

You have her address. As you drive to her house, it strikes you that you don't know the first thing about zombies, nor how to ask a woman if her cousin can turn your soul mate into one. She could say no. She could pretend she doesn't know what you're talking about. Hell, you're not even sure what something like this could cost. You hesitate, almost turn the car around. But you don't.

You walk up her steps. You knock on her door —it is shiny red —and are surprised by the reverberating sound. You peer closer and see the grain of the wood shadowing the cheery paint. You survey the neighboring houses. They are disheveled and well-worn, like clothes from a thrift store. Their doors are stained and discolored. You suspect they are metal. But the door you stand at is no mere entrance. It is a portal.

It opens. An older, more impressive Arvede stares at you. Her hair has gone white and coils on her head like a crown. She wears not an ill-fitting pale green uniform, but a swathe of golds and purples. She looks regal, like her door. "You are not Mr. Christopher," she states.

You say, "Hello, Arvede. It's Henry. From the nursing home." Your voice rises at the end, begging her to remember.

She looks you up and down. Says, "Come back at six." The door shuts. You spend the next three hours in your car, waiting. You swear you hear the beep of machines, slow and steady, like a pulse. You force yourself to think of something else, anything else. Neighbors peer at you from behind wilted curtains. You tell yourself, *I'm not doing anything wrong.*

At six, the red door opens and Arvede exits. You panic, she's leaving before talking to you. But no, she crosses the street and climbs into your car. "Onree," she lilts, "you come for Uti."

You feel relief at not having to explain. Still you try. "I have," you pause, "a friend. He —"

She shushes you. "After dinner. Uti is waiting." She gives you directions. Her heavy scent fills your car, flowery, funereal. You are glad when she points to a parking spot in front of a French bistro and says, "There." You clamber out, open her door.

Inside, Uti waits. He lounges at a table in the center of the restaurant. This time his suit is pale gold. His tie is purple paisley and you feel out of place in your rumpled navy pinstripe. He stands when you and Arvede approach. He smiles and his scars crinkle. Four grins focused at you. He says to his cousin, "You brought a guest. How pleasant." His voice is melodic. His eyes are hungry. Tonight, you are an antelope dining with lions.

"This is Onree," she says and sits. Uti inclines his shaved head at you. You sit. You eat. You fidget under his watchful gaze. Arvede steers the conversation. You talk of food and wine, favorite meals and places. Your mouth aches with words left unsaid, but your stomach swoons with bliss. You have not enjoyed a meal since —ashes coat your tongue. You wash them down with coffee.

"Onree has been a busy boy," Arvede announces. Uti's eyebrows raise. "Our mysterious caller?" You feel your face redden, hope it is not obvious in the ambient lighting. Their eyes rest on you and your tongue is overcome with stage fright. It works in fits and starts. You speak in circles, unsure how to phrase your request. You mention working with Arvede, the coma patients, how your friend was injured, like Mr. Klein —remember Tyler Klein? — you wonder if Uti could consult, if he's not too busy, if perhaps he can do for your friend what he did for Mr. Klein. You stop, unable to read their faces.

As silence stretches across the table, you worry that Arvede is simply a retired housekeeper; that Uti is nothing more than a funeral director; that you've made an ass out of yourself and abandoned the one person whose side you never should've left. You take a deep breath and say, "Will you bring him back?"

Uti laughs, asks "Has he left?" You can't tell if he's denying your request or driving up the price. You're tempted to throw your wallet at him, your car keys, say *take it all, it's yours.* Instead you say, "Please."

Arvede pats your hand. "Onree, it is sad about your David. But do not let sadness push you towards a decision you might regret."

"Mr. Klein walked out of the morgue. Maybe Uti could —" You pause. The image of your love, in a morgue, sheet draped over him, closes your throat.

She tuts. "You were mistaken. That was Mr. Klein's brother."

You look to Uti for his reply. You don't want to push these people, make them think you're a threat. You want to be a client. Just not at their funeral home. You suspect they don't have one.

Uti stares into you, his slashes highlighting his eyes. He asks if you know the story of Jesus Christ and Snow White. You have no idea what he means, you only hear the yes in his words.

He tells you the story. Later you will remember this moment and wish you'd listened. Now, you only hear the parts you want to hear. Death can be undone. David can come home.

You inform the staff you've hired a specialist. You tell his parents you're getting a second opinion before letting him go. Everyone is bewildered; they have questions you won't answer. They ask about certifications and privileges and you say, "Not that kind of doctor, more alternative medicine, experimental." You ramble. A brave soul sends a grief counselor to meet with you. You send her away. You are not grieving. You feel clammy and frenzied and oh so wonderful! You are rejoicing.

Uti comes on a Tuesday. It's the first time you've seen him in the light of day and you realize he's not much older than you. He wears a dove gray suit (the color of his old Cadillac) with a royal blue tie (the color of your love's eyes). He is hatless and carries a walking stick and a black doctor's bag. He looks wise and primal—those matching slashes make your fingers itch. Scents of cinnamon and cloves waft from him, make you think of gingerbread men and sugar plum fairies.

"So this is your prince-child," he says, looking at David. "I see why you don't want to let him go. You know he won't be the same, yes?" His voice slides around the room and slinks into your ear. *This*, you think, *is how the devil whispers.* You nod.

He sets his bag down and looks at you. "Snow White in the movie is not the same Snow White as the story. Everyone wants the movie version, but this is no movie. Snow White is a servant, not some pampered princess, Henry."

"I don't"—you say—"understand."

"Of course you do," he says, thumping the stick against the tiled floor. "I tell you: he won't be the same; you think I mean in his head and yes, that is true. But he won't be a man. No emotion, no *desire*. If you're hoping for a prince, we should not do this. You will be like the bokor, you understand? Like the story?"

You say you understand, but you don't, not really. You're thinking David will come back as a slower version of himself. You have a cousin with Down's Syndrome. You think zombie-David will be like that. Or maybe like a puppy who needs to be trained. You've never had a dog, but you've seen their devotion. You think it's almost love and you've lived with almost love most of your life. Your concern is whether you have to turn off the life support machines for Uti to do his thing. Because if Uti is snowing you and it doesn't work and the machines are off . . . then David is gone for good. But if the machines stay on and Uti fails, you'll still have your visits.

Uti says it's best if you don't know. You tell him, "Go ahead." He takes a little of your blood. "For bonding," he says, and you leave the room.

You take the elevator down to the cafeteria. You should eat, but get a cup of coffee instead. You don't know how long this will take. You stare out the window at the parking lot. Someone sits next to you.

"Excuse me," he says and this man has the same accent as Arvede; Uti's is less pronounced but he's younger, perhaps watched more television. "My father is on the same floor as your friend. I noticed he had a visitor today. A man whose face is marked?"

You don't say anything. You worry this stranger will report you to the nurses, get you and Uti thrown out.

"I wondered if that man's name was Dupre."

He knows. This man knows what you're planning. You say, "I believe so. He works for a funeral home someone recommended to me."

"It might be best to choose another place."

You question the man: has he heard something, does he know something, is there a problem?

He looks at you and shakes his head. You gave yourself away; you're not sure how. He stands and turns, then turns back to you as if he can't help himself. He says, "Some men enslave the living, others the dead. The Dupres, they do both."

He means to scare you, to change your mind. Instead you feel better about your decision. The man said *Dupres*, in the plural, which means the family is experienced at zombie-making, they're renowned.

You finish your coffee, then head back. In the elevator, it occurs to you that you never wondered what happened to Mr. Klein once he left. He'd gone with Uti, not his family. You hurry down the hall, worried Uti might steal David, although you're not sure for what purpose. You burst through the door and both are still there. So is Arvede, which is unexpected. The Dupres are bent over David. They wear latex gloves, except for Uti's left hand which holds his stick. Uti waves the stick in the air above the bed. The room smells like church on Easter. Thoughts of the Jesus Christ in Uti's story try to haunt you. You banish them.

Arvede gestures for you to come close; Uti scowls at her. She holds a carved bowl with some goopy mixture in it. She says, "Scoop some up and smear on his lips and tongue." You do as you're told. It is reddish black on your finger, it feels like lumpy mud. She whispers, "Tell him to wake."

You say, "Wake up." It echoes in the room. David's eyes fly open. You tear up.

Arvede doesn't look at you. She's packing things into a bag of her own. She says, "If you change your mind, Onree, give him a little salt and it will be done." You recall this from the story Uti told you. Salt returns the zombie to the grave. You thought it fiction. This bit of truth tucked into a legend bothers you, like a buzzing fly. You swat the feeling away.

Before he leaves, Uti says, "You don't need to feed him. You can if you want, but it is unnecessary and the result is messy. If you do, nothing with salt. It'd be best if you sealed his mouth shut, to prevent any accidents. Unless, of course, you want to use it for other things."

You pretend to not hear him. He continues, "A little surgical glue on the back edge of the lips works best. Looks natural and gives them fuller lips."

Uti takes your hand in his. His grip startles you. His skin is softer than you imagined. It makes you daydream about those scars under your fingertips. Then he says,

"Henry, if things do not work out, I'd be happy to take your Snow White off your hands. Sometimes it's harder if you knew them before." Uti hands you a card with an address on it. You flip it over and see a number scrawled on the back.

"Call me," he says, "if you have questions. Or another body." The payment you agreed upon for David's resurrection is seven men, no older than thirty, preferably younger, preferably alive. "Higher success rate with the living," Uti said. "They retain more, are easier to transfer control." You already have ideas where to find them.

You stick the card in a pocket and wait until they've cleared the building. Then you buzz for a nurse. You tell yourself, *This will work.* You tell yourself, *Get him out of here before they give him salt.* You tell David, "Sit up." He sits.

His parents visit. They ask, "What is that smell? Is someone burning incense?" Whatever Arvede and Uti did, the smell of frankincense and myrrh permeate David's skin no matter how hard he's sponged. You tell his parents, "It's David's favorite cologne. I gave it to him last Christmas."

They suggest he stay in the home. They offer to pay for his care. You show them how much progress David's made, you get the staff to praise his recovery. David doesn't say anything at all. He can't. But he understands your words, your commands. His parents look at you like you're a demented monster. They don't look at David at all. Someone, that damn doctor, must have mentioned the lack of brain waves to them. Or maybe it was the nurse who caught you flushing his dinner down the drain.

You tell them, "David's going home today. I have every-thing ready." You've zombie-proofed your home: child latches on kitchen cabinets, padlock on the fridge.

You monologue the entire ride home, catching David up on the latest gossip. You point out landmarks and street names. You ask if he wants to go the movies tonight. You take his silence as agreement.

Once inside the house, you hug him. He doesn't hug you back. You place his arms around you and tell him to hold tight. He does.

You give bags of Sno-Melt to the neighbors. You'll use kitty-litter or sand—that has to be sodium-free, right? You go on a no-salt diet, read labels in the supermarket like they're legal contracts you're thinking of signing. You watch David like a hawk, afraid he'll shove things in his mouth at every opportunity like a baby. Eventually, like any new mother, you relax. He doesn't do anything unless you tell him. But you have to be specific. Yesterday you told him to go watch television while you worked on the computer. Hours later you found him sitting in a dark room, staring at a blank screen. You turned on the t.v. and sat next to him. Put your arm around him, molded him to your body. You told yourself, *He'll learn.*

You don't mind that he doesn't talk. You find it almost refreshing. You became used to his silence all those hours you spent beside his hospital bed. Sometimes he grunts and once you thought you heard him moan. But maybe that was you.

He's more considerate now and your house has never been so clean. He doesn't complain about picking up socks or scrubbing floors. Although you don't ask him to take out the garbage. That chore you keep.

He doesn't sleep, but you coach him to curl on the bed next to you while you do. He is warm and pliable. You've gotten used to his Easter scent, even like its taste when you kiss. Although some nights you dream of cinnamon-and-clove-scented skin, wake with a knowing chuckle echoing in your ear. You like the way David kisses now better, the way you've showed him, yet there are times you wish he'd overwhelm you with passion, like he used to. But at least you don't have to worry about him straying.

Winter comes. You stop taking David out in public. People watch as you lead him by the hand. They ask if he's your brother. At first you said, "No, boyfriend." But you didn't like the looks that got you. So then you said cousin. Now you don't want anyone to see him with you. This perfectly biddable, blank-faced yet still fucking gorgeous Snow White.

You pull out the card Uti gave you and stare at the number. You have both it and the address memorized. You want to call him, have a conversation with a good-looking man who will respond. But you need an excuse, because what if he isn't interested in you that way. You owe him seven strangers. Maybe you should get started on that.

You dress David up, bring him to a club. You hate driving in the city, but need your own transportation. The bouncer asks if David's on something. You tell him it's H and he lets you pass. The music is loud and rhythmic. For a second you're reminded of beeping machines and hissing ventilators. You snap out of it. You position David near the bar where he can draw the most attention. He's your dwarf-bait.

You almost forget why you're there. You're enjoying yourself, except when the bartender mixes a margarita or fixes a tequila shot. After each order, you rub David's hands, checking for grains of salt. But this is habit for you and each time they come away clean.

You spot your targets and whisper in David's ear, then follow him to where they are. They look at David with greedy eyes. It's easy to convince them to come home with you.

You call Uti. He sounds glad to hear from you and you chat. You tell him about your night out. He says the two of you should go out together one evening, if you're up for it. He knows this great place. You mention you have three bodies for him. He says, "Henry, you've been busy."

Uti plays with the buttons on your shirt while David loads the drugged men into the hearse. You close your eyes and will him to slip the buttons from their loops. He doesn't, but you enjoy the teasing. He says, "Your Snow White is very well trained. When you called, I thought perhaps you were returning him." You wonder if Uti's more interested in sex with David than you. Anger at David for ruining your moment rips through you. You almost order him into the hearse. But then your head clears. You tell yourself, *You can't cheat on David. You love him.* Still, lust follows Uti's loaded hearse down your driveway. You wish you'd licked his scars.

You stop talking to David. Before you'd chat about your day or tell him stories or how to do things. But you've run out of things to show him and he's never going to respond, no matter how hard you try to teach him to speak or force him to remember times you had together.

The constant silence grates on you. You leave the t.v. on and pretend you're eavesdropping on other people's conversations. You miss talking to someone. You wonder what Uti is doing.

If David wasn't around, you'd be free to be with Uti. There are so many things you can't do because of David. Loving zombie-David isn't the same. He looks like David, but your love's not in there. Those men from the club would've been happy fucking this David and that pisses you off. Because why can't you be happy? Why do you keep wishing for more? Arvede's words snake across your brain: *Give him a little salt and it will be done.*

If it weren't for David, you could eat whatever you wanted instead of tasteless crap. You want nothing more than to stuff French fries into your mouth. The salt, the grease, you crave it. You tell David to go to his room. Outside, it's flurrying. Flakes coat your eyelashes and dot your coat. You drive the car to the nearest drive-thru. Sit in the parking lot and eat and it tastes oh so good. You stuff fries and burger into your mouth, moaning at each bite.

You finish way too quickly, considering driving around again, maybe going inside this time. The grit of salt on your fingers distracts you. You imagine pushing them into David's mouth. His last supper. You wonder if he will keel over at the first lick or if he will suck all five fingers before succumbing to that final sleep.

You make it home and into the house before your resolution turns to horror. You can't kill David. You race for the kitchen and wash away the salt and your murderous thoughts in hot, hot water until your skin is red and swollen. He stands behind you waiting for your instruction. Go rake the goddamn yard, you yell and he shuffles out before you remember it's snowing. You watch him rake at the ground, creating furrows in the snow. He isn't wearing a coat. You tell yourself, *This can't go on.*

Yet the kitchen countertops gleam, the grout sparkles. David scoured it with a toothbrush. Eight hours on his knees; they oozed a sticky yellowish sap when he finished, a reminder that zombie-David isn't completely human. If you think about it too hard, you'll realize he's your slave. You've bought him with a down payment of three souls. *Some men enslave the living, others the dead. The Dupres do both.*

You stare at him. You used to watch to ensure he didn't hurt himself, now you hope he does. You think about Jesus Christ and Snow White as you wait for an accident to happen. You curse the Dupres. Why aren't there three of them? Because then, maybe, you'd have a Jesus Christ instead of a Snow White. When you first heard the tale, a Snow White sounded fine, better than nothing, but now you have Snow White and you want Jesus.

"While any bokor can separate a man's essence from his shell," Uti told you, "it takes three powerful bokors to bind and return it to the shell. They say the spell requires three days, a gilded soul, the consent of the night sky, royal blood and spices of the resurrection."

Not that you believe the three wise men were bokors who purchased a prince-child's soul with gold and promissory spices, then returned thirty-three years later to collect their prize. Uti's Jesus didn't ascend into heaven; he went to Africa. On their way home, his makers quarreled over who owned him. While they fought, Jesus traded spices with a shepherd, fragrant for cooking. He then salted his tongue, freeing his soul and laying his shell to rest. Two of the bokors joined him in death. The third forsook their spell. Talking, thinking zombies made bad slaves.

In Uti's story, Snow White, Sleeping Beauty and Cinderella are one person. She starts as Snow White who runs away rather than marry the third bokor. The spurned bokor finds her and tricks her into drinking a potion that mimics death. His beauty sleeps while he revises his spell. To avoid another catastrophe, he seals her soul in a mirror. When she is re-awakened, she is the shell of herself—Cinderella —the perfect wife who can only do what she is told.

There is no happily ever after.
You call your bokor.

It's Arvede who comes. She leads David to her car like he's a child, straps him into the passenger seat, and returns to speak with you. You'd rather she just drive off. You don't want to know where she's taking him or what will happen. Maybe she'll feed him salt, maybe she'll sell him. Just don't let her give him to Uti. You realize how gut-wrenching it would've been if you had to see the two of them drive off together. This way's better. You say, "Thank you." Press a packet of salt into her hands.

She smiles. Says, "You a good man, Onree." She tilts her head and adds, "But maybe you'd make a better bokor."

Be Careful What You Wish For

~ *Jetse de Vries*

In the early 2030s, over a period of several weeks, Shenzhen *shifted*. Already China's hotbed of the rapidly developing electronics and synthetic biology sector and an industrial juggernaut at large, it was a fierce focal point of both piracy and innovation. Unrestrained by intellectual property and restrictive regulations, the *shanzhai* conglomeration's pace of innovation accelerated, and as they also innovated their own production methods, the acceleration accelerated. Its technological development became a blur and Shenzhen shifted into what is now referred to as SIS, an acronym whose meaning—Shenzhen Innovation Swarm? Shenzhen Infodump Swamp? Shenzhen's Iteration Storm?—remained elusive, just as what exactly is happening within it.

As such, it became a higher dimensional space within a space, an ineffable knowledge state within a state, a hyper-culture within a culture. Everything within it goes so fast, only a true SIS-citizen can keep up. Everything enveloped by it is so strange, only the weird SISters can understand it. Everything developed inside it so advanced, only the actual SIS-tems know how to use it. As on old maps, the unknown area is marked as 'Here Be Dragons.' A veritable fountainhead of innovation where raw materials entered and futuristic gadgets, computing extravaganzas and programmable monsters—years ahead of their time—exited.

The Chinese authorities were caught by surprise and remained frozen in indecision. On the one hand, they didn't want to kill the goose that laid the golden innovation eggs; on the other hand, they felt they'd completely lost control over it. Somehow, SIS generates its own energy and is an irresistible siren song to nerds, geeks and entrepreneurs across both China and the world at large. But SIS does need an input of raw materials, which the Chinese authorities—and countries and companies worldwide, through what used to be Shenzhen's sea port—but all too gladly provide, as the output is a veritable cornucopia of hardware gadgets, software apps or a combination thereof that was years ahead of the competition.

In the end, the Chinese authorities remained practical: as long as they got their cut of the SIS pie, and as long as that remained an important part of China's economical growth, it could go on as a 'special administrative region' in a similar manner that neighbouring Hong Kong and Macau already had been doing. It wasn't as if anybody outside of China had the faintest clue of what was going on, as well.

☉

Aiguo Zhang is an agent of the MSS, a man who truly believes in everything China stands for. He has a PhD in computer science from Tsinghua University and a BA in applied molecular biology. He fondles his wooden Yin & Yang amulet, the last present his mother gave him before she unexpectedly died. He stands at the very edge of the SIS zone, where a local guide will pick him up. From out of nowhere, an entity appears. Zhang needs all his restraint not to run away in terror, as the entity resembles a Feng creature with the jaws of a dragon. "Don't fear, good citizen," the abomination says. "We just needed to clean up a synthetic biology experiment that had gotten a little bit out of hand."

Frozen in fear and indecision, Zhang can only manage: "A *little* bit out of hand?"

"Don't pay attention to my external appearance, as it's merely ephemeral." The hump of unidentified flesh says through its dragon mouth. "Let's go in and join the fun." The left-hand side extruding piece of meat moves with a 'come-with-me' motion, the right-hand side extruding piece of meat appendage holds, for whatever reason, a whip. Zhang has no choice but to follow. Through a twilight zone they enter a blurry world where everything just moves and happens faster.

"We're in the zone now, so we can choose decent transportation," the creature, who's shape-shifting into a kind of insect heap, says, "anyway, welcome to Über-Shanzhai."

"Über-Shanzhai?" Zhang says, "I thought this was called SIS."

"SIS is just a placeholder for those not in the know," the creature says, "it's time to design your transportation." In the meantime, contraptions that defy description pass by at speeds varying from stupidly fast to utterly insane. Somehow, they manage not to barrel into Zhang and his local companion.

"But what do I call you?" Zhang wants some certainty in this utter chaos.

"I'm Positive Feedback Loop Entity Alpha Pi Tango 888-bis," the entity says, "but my friends call me FleaPit, unless they think I'm FlyLord, in which case they call me BeetleDung."

"OK, well, FleaPit, I'm Aiguo Zhang." Zhang tries to concentrate. "Is there something like a bus or a train here? Maybe even a metro?"

"Are you crazy?" The laugh coming from the dragon mouth belches fire. "We've grown way beyond those medieval, authoritarian means of transport. No, we make it up on the fly. Feel free to go ahead."

Zhang is at a loss. "How?"

"Well, we brainstorm the design of your über-transportation. What would you prefer: a swarm of drones? A constantly shape-shifting blip in turbulent joyride mode? A slithering ground-snake with an ever-changing, interestingly-smelling lubricant (colour and glow-in-the-dark optional)? A thunderbolt-driven porcupined hedge-hodgepodge?" FleaPit gloats as it lists up alternatives. "But don't let my humble hints limit your imagination."

"You mean that we can just order a complete new means of transportation like that?" Zhang says in utter disbelief. "Like a self-levitating pod with a continuous track of superconducting coils?"

"Consider it done," FleaPit says, "Our mega-flexible and ultrafast production lines will have them delivered in no time." FleaPit unleashes its whip, which hits Zhang on the shoulder. "*Pull über push!*"

Zhang is too stunned to react.

"BTW, are you still a man?" FleaPit asks as they wait for their transport, "Did you have your hourly sex-change yet? The possibilities are endless, and the first six are on the house. It'll loosen you up, and make you fit in here that much easier."

"I'm not sure if I really—" Zhang is interrupted by the arrival of a pod levitating atop a continuous track that alternately pulls and pushes with a vehement force on his smartphone, smartwatch and smart earrings.

"I took the liberty of implementing your bio-adaptation," FleaPit says. "It's the least I could do for an honorable guest with such an exquisite taste in transportation."

Zhang wants to protest but screams in pain as his smartphone, smartwatch and smart earrings heat up and eventually melt in the onslaught of the rapidly pulsating electromagnetic fields of the superconducting continuous track. Thank dog his Yin & Yang amulet remains intact. FleaPit, who now metamorphoses from flesh hump to insect swarm devouring the flesh hump, laughs it off.

"They forgot to implement a Faraday Cage in the pod housing," FleaPit guffaws as Zhang's gadgets melt away from him, "but you know how it is," FleaPit lashes his whip against the pod's roof, *"practice über theory!"*

"But it hurts," Zhang says, his voice rising at least an octave. His head of hair grows out, his breasts expand, his waist narrows and his reproductive organs reform as muscle, fat and other flesh are re-arranged throughout his body. "And I'm becoming a woman." She says with a mix of disbelief and terror.

"A charming one, at that." FleaPit, who now resembles a colony of insects crawling over rotting flesh, says.

"But my phone, my watch, my smart jewellery," the female Zhang says. "They're toast."

"Your pre-historical gadgets are damaged beyond repair," it says through snorting giggles, "but they were useless here, anyway, and slumbering clumps of metal and plastic most of the time you weren't using them. Allow me to introduce you to our cloud-based interfaces. Fear not, they will adapt and improve as they absorb your quirky personal preferences. Obviously, the cloud will not remain static, but is already evolving beyond something like mere cloudiness. Gone are those good old days of MicroGoogølBook and SoftFaceFruit, welcome to the era of the continuously improving megaweb which cannot be named as its name changes faster than it can be pronounced. The IT, the id, the bit-to-byte, the sod-it-unmentionable." With a quick flick of the wrist, FleaPit lashes its whip at an ever-moving sky. *"Systems über objects!"*

"First you were a Feng with dragon jaws, now you look like an insect-infested carcass," Zhang struggles to keep up. "How do I know you are still the same, well, entity that picked me up at the edge?"

"Does it matter? My external form is still comprised of mostly the same atoms, while my mind constantly evolves. I suppose my spirit is more-or-less the same, but who can tell? Who cares?" FleaPit cracks the whip, which lashes around Zhang's now hairless wrist, surprisingly gently. "*Compasses über maps!*"

They arrive at some place that might somewhat resemble a plaza or a food court, if most of it would just stay in focus. "Time for a tea," Fleapit says, "as we outsource your amusement."

"Yes, FleaPit." Zhang nods in agreement. "I could use a simple tea."

"I'm not FleaPit anymore," the entity previously known as FleaPit says, "I've moved to FlyLord."

Zhang has to admit that many of post-FleaPit's characteristics have metamorphosed into the Diptera realm. "OK, I suppose," Zhang says. "And the tea?"

"Indeed," FlyLord says, "how about a fresh yellow? Junshan Yinzhen?"

"Actually, if you could be so kind," Zhang says, "I'd rather prefer a soothing green, like a West Lake Dragon Well?"

"Fine," FlyLord says as it signals for the waiter. With a flash and a bang, a robotic contraption somewhere between The Shrike and a Battlemech of Maximum Tech explodes right next to Zhang's and FlyLord's table.

"You wished to order?" It voices in a hyperfast, mechanical shriek.

"Indeed," FlyLord says, as flies of its colony gobble up flies, becoming bigger. "A fine white one, say a Silver Needle?"

"Two White Peony's coming up," the waiter, who now evokes shadows of Darth Vader says before it leaves the scene with an asthmatic growl.

Before Zhang can protest, the mecha-waiter is gone. Within seconds, though, it's back with the order. "Here's your Keemun Experimental House Reserve," as it places the black tea in front of FlyLord, "and here's your Wenshan Baozhong Special Batch." As it places the Oolong tea in front of Zhang.

Zhang wants to roll her eyes, but fondles her Yin & Yang amulet and just gives up.

"Excellent." FlyLord says while two of its six legs groom its transparent wings, *"Disobedience über compliance!"*

Reluctantly, Zhang tastes her tea. Contrary to her worst fears, it's quite good. "It's difficult to define in a good way," she says, "it's got all the hallmarks of a classic Wenshan Baozhong, yet there are exciting extras. Quite interesting."

"It took some time," FlyLord says, "but we're increasingly finding teahouses willing to experiment with our synthetic biology recipes."

"Willing to engage in Future Shock?" Zhang, remembering a classic.

"Future Shock?" FlyLord says, "How quaint. We considered that a 'how-not-to.'"

"That tea was quite good," Zhang says, "but now I feel like I have a double need to pee."

"Which you indeed might." FlyLord flashes a sardonic, insectoid smile.

Zhang looks at FlyLord in disbelief, then carefully touches her—correct that, ber—nether regions. Yes, both male and female reproductive organs. "What the hell, I'm a hermaphrodite!"

"Well, that took long enough," FlyLord says, "but it'll speed up your unproductive waste release by a factor of two."

Zhang asks for directions to the toilet and goes there, before thoughts of how to pee from two organs at once and the idea of what toilets might actually look like in this indefinable zone might stop ber.

Be comes back, mission accomplished—don't ask how—and faces an entity like a swarm of beetles crawling over something pungent that's better not described. Still, Zhang is fairly sure this is where be came from.

"It's OK," the entity says, "it's me, BeetleDung."

"I thought you were FlyLord?"

"FlyLord is so last minute," the entity stretches its half-domed wings, "BeetleDung is where it's at." From somewhere inside the myriad of creepy-crawlies, a whip lashes around the insect mound. *"Diversity über ability!"*

Zhang wants to say something, but is distracted by the constant *'Zzzzip-Dong/Zzzzip-Dong/Zzzzip-Dong'* sound that seems to come from somewhere close by. "What's that irritating sound?"

"That's just your sex becoming volatile," BeetleDung says, "While you were enjoying your tea, our cloud-but-not-quite-cloud estimated your taste, preference and sense of humour. Experience your tailor-made performance."

While fe didn't pay attention, a whole mini-cinema-cum-street-theatre was erected behind Zhang. A mix of actual actors and projected entities perform a play/sitcom/vignette/newscast whose topics, tone and subject change just as quick as the actors—virtual, real or augmented—change appearance. It's fast, furious and almost over before it begins.

"This doesn't work," Zhang says, needing no hormones to express fis utter disagreement, "the narrative is a jumbles, the tone is inconsistent, the theme so thoroughly unthematic it gives Dadaists migraines."

"It didn't work for you?" The disappointment is unmistakable in BeetleDung's voice. "Too bad."

"Bad's the word," flashing Zhang says, "godawfully bad."

"They win now, a Pyrrhic victory," BeetleDung says, "but we will bounce back, as we always will, like the ever-improving army of phoenixes that we are." It lashes its whip at a giant sign that flashes from Hollywood to Bollywood to Shollywood. "*Resilience über strength!*"

"I feel strange, BeetleDung," Zhang says, "as if I'm locked in."

"BeetleDung is last minute's news," an entity so overwhelmed with insect-like appendages it resembles an insect god, says, "InsectIDecide feels much better. Shift for the moment."

"I'm sweating like a pig," Zhang says, "Normally, I never do that. What gives?"

"Because you're a neuter now, your sexual organs have been obliterated," InsectIDecide says, "so to get rid of your excess liquids you need to sweat."

"I need to perspire my superfluous fluids?" Zhang says in despair, "So that's why they smell so funny. Now I'm afraid to eat."

"No problem," InsectIDecide says, "we can design food whose waste will crawl back from whence it cameth. Our marketing cloud suggests 'Vomitorium Automaticum.'"

"I think I'll eat tomorrow," Zhang says, ner face a paler shade of yellow, "after I've acclimatised a little."

"You sure?" InsectIDecide says, "Our cuisine is so much more interesting than the dull stuff they serve on the mainland. On your plate as soon as it's made."

"There's no authority testing your food?" Zhang says, fearing the answer. "Food safety is important, you know."

"Of course not," InsectIDecide says, "that would only hold back innovation. It's never the same, like your thoughts, your whims, your sex." Seemingly out of nowhere, its whip lashes dangerously close to Zhang's nether regions. "*Risk über safety!*"

Utterly overwhelmed, Zhang doesn't even bother to check what the hell is happening between nis legs. "I'm tired, I need a place to sleep," Ne says, fearing the answer. "Do you have anything resembling a hotel here?"

"Not really," InsectIDecide says, "but we can manufacture one for you on the fly."

"OK," Zhang says, accepting the inevitable, "but make sure it has a decent bed."

"No problem," InsectIDecide says. "It'll be the most innovative bed you've ever slept in, and probably will ever sleep in."

"I'm pwned and tired beyond my wits," Zhang says, "so I need a good night's rest."

"Of course, the bed you'll wake up in will be different from the bed you went to sleep in," InsectIDecide says. "If you're lucky it has remained mostly a bed in between. It'll have to do until you learn to ignore sleep."

"Ignore sleep?" Zhang asks, against ner better judgement.

"And similar minor distractions like sex, drugs, alcohol and other earthly diversions," InsectIDecide says, unleashing its whip at a structure behind Zhang. "*Emergence über authority!*"

Zhang turns around, and isn't even surprised to see that a one-bedroom hotel has arisen while ne talked with InsectIDecide who increasingly morphs into a giant moth. "See you later," ne says, strokes ner Yin & Yang amulet for luck and gets into nis personal hotel.

Inside, the bed is surprisingly good. Zhang undresses, decides not to check what's happening between ner legs and almost immediately falls in a deep sleep. But not quite dreamless.

☉

Zhang's in a Realm where bleeding edge, constantly modifying production lines, effervescent synthetic biology labs and berserk coding parlours are but the baseline of the madness arising from them. A veritable transformocracy where flash-adaptation reigns supreme. A parade of paradigm shifts conceptually breaking through boundaries like tachyons through time. A software nirvana where code transcends context, consistency and conditions. The place where change goes to change. The realm where reality surpasses the real. The commonality that condemns common sense.

Zhang gives up trying to cope with it. *Let it be*, ne thinks, *go with the flow*. As ne lets go, nis vision enhances and ner sense of time speeds up. Slowly—no, scratch that—quickly the pieces fall into place, and a vision surfaces. If 'Here Be Dragons,' then it's best to ride these dragons. But how do you control them?

InsectIDecide's whip is key, Zhang now sees. The beautiful, Art Nouveau-styled reverse ellipses as it travels through the air. The short, sharp crack of pain and revelation as it hits. This is how the truly innovative hits the unsuspecting newcomer—unexpected, painful at first but with a sense of wonder and sheer efficiency as its meaning slams home. Why invent so painstakingly slow when you can unleash the new with a snap that makes Future Shock seem like small fry? Whiplash is the true way forward!

Innovation. Embrace-the-new. Novophilia Supreme. The whiplashtic fantastic.

- Of course using latent resources is better than producing dead stock—*Pull über push!*
- Creativity must not be constrained, but rather encouraged, nay, spread like a benevolent and contagious virus—*Disobedience über compliance!*
- Why spend years in education if you can fiddle, tweak and improvise until it works? *Practice über theory!*
- Don't get stuck in a rut of compliance, but innovate or die—*Risk über safety!*
- Use everything, and that means literally absolutely everything you've got and can get your hands on—*Diversity über ability!*
- Never give up, never give in, never say never again—*Resilience über strength!*
- Don't try to draw the path you'll be taking beforehand, as it limits the real paths you can take—*Compasses über maps!*
- The polyphonic subject: all feelings are mixed, all thoughts are shared, all deeds are collective—*Emergence über authority!*
- Our brains and the world at large are loci of overlapping systems, not singular objects in themselves—*Systems über objects!*

The hotel around nim has disappeared. Zhang nerself has become a motørcyborg on two wheels, with miniature exhaust pipes emerging through its sideburns. "Hello

MothRa," Novo-Zhang says, polishing its exhaust pipes, "I feel much better now. Better, tauter, faster than before."

"You know my new name. You're finally getting the hang of it." The giant moth with the aura of a Sun God says.

"It was written all over you. Now we must hurry up," Novo-Zhang says, "so much to invent, so little time."

"Speed is of the essence," MothRa says, "*Über über essence!*"

Their words and actions become entangled in one big razzamatazz of innovation mumbo jumbo, hypertechno patois and *shanzhai* jargon which changes almost as fast as they can pronounce it . . .

Carrie-Anne Piscatore is an agent of the CIA, a woman who truly believes in everything America stands for. She has a PhD in synthetic biology and a BA in applied mechatronics. She stands at the very edge of the SIS zone, where a local guide will pick her up. She fondles her wedding ring, thinking of her husband. From out of nowhere, an entity appears. Piscatore needs all her reserves of willpower not to scream in terror, as the entity resembles a walking atomic bomb with the head of Peter Sellers whose mouth has the shape of a rocket launcher. The whole contraption is enveloped with a radioactive sheen, glowing menacingly. "Don't be afraid, good guest," the monstrosity says. "We needed to clean up after we somewhat overestimated the critical mass of a nuclear-charged widget."

Biting through a stupor of pure fear and sick fascination, Piscatore says: "Only *somewhat*?"

"Please ignore my outer shell, it's only temporary," the radioactive nightmare from Hell says through its rocket-launcher mouth. "Come in and join the fun." Atomic Sellers's left hand gestures to follow it, while its right hand holds, for whatever reason, a whip. A wooden Yin & Yang amulet hangs from a cord around its neck. Piscatore has no choice but to follow.

VIII

Wolf's Clothing

~ *Jonathan Wood*

The sheep's mind closing over Sean's, snug as a wool coat. A sensation of womb-like envelopment. His vision flushing red as he invades orbital nerves. Wind rushing over his back, and the loamy scent of fresh mountain grass shuddering into his nostrils as the parietal lobe is overwritten. Frontal cortex stretching to accommodate him, tight as a sock fresh from the dryer.

Elsewhere, his body releases an involuntary grunt of satisfaction. Here, a wooly bleat emerges from a foreign mouth.

Sean blinks. The sheep blinks. They blink. All the seams between the two of them erased.

Mindjack complete.

For a moment, he just stands there, takes it in: the wind-swept hillside, the ochre grass, a slate sky tousled with scudding clouds, trees jostling up the slope to the north. And the flock. The thick white press of bodies on all sides. The soft slug of dopamine as this body relishes its place among them.

Then the others come gamboling across the hillside toward him, mouths wide in shrill bleats of joy. Ali, Jazz, and Kai unsteady as newborns, bucking like lambs with the sheer glory of this rebirth. The older ewes in the flock staring at them dully, then lowering their heads to shovel up the dry stalks once more.

Sean bumbles and bustles with his friends, the group battering these bodies against each other in softly cushioned delight. He rolls onto his back, kicking all four of his absurd, stubby legs in the air. He nips and sniffs at his friends; runs in wobbling, unsteady glory, charging for the woods, letting the scent of pine and danger flood him until his whole sheep-body shivers with it. He eats grass, feels it foreign between molars grown massive and powerful, feels the dull satisfaction of grinding his way to a full belly. Across the field, Kai and Jazz screw, ungainly and urgent. Ali rolls her rectangular pupils heaven-ward.

Then, with a shudder and a shake, it's over. Sean dumped unceremoniously back into the meat of himself; plucking tacky electrodes from his forehead; clambering out of the booth with a slight tremor in his limbs.

"Drinks?" Kai's grin is still vaguely ovine.

They started mindjacking sheep two months back. When they'd first started out, they'd done birds. Everybody did birds. It was a cliché. They'd been clichés. Bald eagles. Golden ones. Then Osprey. Then Andean Condors, sailing thermals for miles, barely flapping their wings the whole time they rented the booth. Next: red-tailed kites; sparrowhawks; a wild, wild night as peregrine falcons, and Ali still swearing blind she threw up feathers the next day. Getting more esoteric as they descended deeper into the scene. Antioquia brushfinches. Blue-eyed ground-doves. One night, just plain old house sparrows.

From there they'd graduated to predators. Bears first, massive and shaggy in the woods, stomping about feeling fecund and feral. That's when Sean had finally hooked up with Ali. Kai and Jazz had been together since before the scene, Ali and Sean orbiting their passion. And Sean had yearned, but never said anything.

"She's into you, man." Kai's mantra as they'd take the subway back to Brooklyn every week. Sean always denied it, but, yeah, she'd been into him. And sitting in a bear's body all the things he couldn't say to her in his own skin hadn't needed to be said anymore. They'd just crashed into each other, jaws, and claws, and fur.

After bears: lions and tigers, oh my. Learning to love the stringy feeling of game in their jaws.

Most people in the scene found something they loved after a year or so. Some animal that filled the hole they were trying to fill. Their "regulars." Then they'd start getting specific. They didn't want to be a crow, but a fish crow, or a pied crow, or a you-didn't-even-know-they-made-that-flavor-of-crow crow. But Sean and the others had never settled, never gone back to a body more than twice before moving on, restless as nomads.

And then Jazz had said, "What about sheep?"

It was a joke, of course. Nobody did sheep. You could be anything. You did this to shake off the world. To be red of tooth and claw. To rediscover life in its natural state. That what all the ads said, what all the articles were about, what all the TV pundits fretted over. You did this to shed the sheeple stink from your skin. Who would mindjack a sheep?

Which is why they did it. Because it wasn't done. Because it was transgressive, which was half the fun, wasn't it? And as Sean felt the sheep's mind close over his, something about it had just felt . . . right.

"Simplicity." That had been Ali's first word when they gathered outside the pods. And that had been it exactly, and he'd kissed her hard and deep, and it had just been . . . right.

"They want me to work late tonight."

Ali across the table in their postage stamp apartment, examining her pop tart like a dissection in high school biology. Sean warming his hands on his coffee.

"But it's Wednesday." They always 'jacked on Wednesdays. Religiously.

"We need the money."

"You need the break." Sean disguising his interests as hers; immediately undermining the move by saying, "Can't you work late tomorrow?"

A grimace. Her nose wrinkling. He wants to kiss her. Because he knows she wants to 'jack as much as he does. That this is really her way of asking him to workshop an excuse.

"Tell them you have a class tonight. Something about digital design in the neural age." Ali's advertising executive superiors will like that, surely.

She laughs a little in her throat, and he shivers at the sound of it. She pulls his hands off the coffee mug, slides hers into them.

"Mmm, warm."

The pleather lining of the booth still hot from the previous user. The sharp smell of the alcohol wipe that Sean uses to clean his forehead. The electrodes in all their familiar places. He closes his eyes-

-opens them elsewhere. Feels his body dissolve, another take its place. Releases a happy bleat.

The flock has moved higher up the hillside. The grass is fresher here. He shovels it down, Ali stands next to him, chewing cud, dreamy-eyed. Jazz and Kai are a few yards away frolicking with one of the lambs. Kai told him, standing in line at the bodega sandwich counter for lunch, that they've started talking about kids.

When the change comes, Sean feels it without understanding it. A shudder that runs through the whole flock. Bodies aligning themselves like iron filings in a magnetic field. A quiver in his skin.

It stands against the tree line. A body low-slung. Powerful limbs. Yellow eyes sunk deep in black fur.

Wolves, he thinks. *How have we never been wolves?*

Then it comes, rushing, snarling. The flock leaps as one unit, fleeing pell-mell, slaves to terror and the urge of self-preservation.

Except four sheep do not turn as smoothly as the rest. Four respond to the flock instinct just a second slower. Four are not quite as comfortable in the bodies that they must now make sprint flat out in a race to survive.

The wolf among them. Stronger than them. Faster than them. More savage than them.

It's a second before Sean realizes Ali isn't next to him anymore. He's still running, body bouncing with terror, the fear a hard fist in him. Then the absence registers. Human instincts override the animal urge. He skids to a stop, falls, picks himself up with a clatter of limbs, and turns back.

The wolf has her by the throat. Blood pours down her white fleece, the life going dim in her pleading eyes.

Sean discovers that a sheep can scream.

The wolf twists its head. Ali's throat comes away with a long, wet rip. She drops limp. Sean bucks forward.

And then it's over. Times up. Sean isn't a sheep anymore. He's a sweaty twenty-something in a sticky pleather booth.

Sean tearing himself out of the machine. Nausea rising. Jazz already in the corridor outside, doubled over, rediscovering religion. "Oh Jesus. Oh Jesus. Oh Jesus." Kai stumbles out after her, vomits onto the floor.

"Ali," Sean says. She hasn't come out of the booth.

He almost tears the booth door off its hinges. She's lying there.

Death can happen while you're 'jacked, of course. Hell, it's why some people do it. A dark part of the scene—not their part of the scene—but they know about it. It's just never happened to them before. Hell, the whole point of sheep is how mellow they are.

"Ali!" He's almost screaming.

She turns and looks at him, and he almost collapses in relief.

She doesn't say anything the whole subway ride home. The guy at the front desk told them that'd be normal, said she'd be fine in a bit, recommends chicken soup.

The rest of them more than make up for her silence, fill the train car with anxious jittery words, repeating, and recycling, and recontextualizing the event over and over. Sean holds Ali's hand in his. It feels warm. Alive. Thank God. He keeps flashing back to it: the look in the wolf's eyes as it tore the life out of her.

She doesn't stand up when the train pulls into their station.

"Hey, Ali." He reaches down to help her.

She snarls at him.

He steps back, alarmed

She keeps staring at him, teeth bared, a growl in the back of her throat.

"Ali . . . ?" All three of them staring at her.

Then Kai starts to grin. "Oh man, you had me-"

She dives at him. A liquid unfurling from the bench seat. A leaping spring and Ali crashes full-bodied into Kai, sends him flailing him backward, head crashing into the pole, spinning him around, and sending him dazedly to the floor. Then she's on him, scrambling over him, feet and hands grinding against thigh, chest, forearm. Kai yells. Sean yells. People yell as they jump out of the car, and the doors start to shrill closed.

Ali closing her teeth over Kai's throat.

Sean thinks he's going to throw up.

The train starts to rumble out of the station. Escape paths shutting down. Dull-eyed panic taking hold. Then someone grabs the emergency cord, and they're all flung off balance as the train grinds to a screaming, terrified halt.

Ali is flung off Kai. She still has her teeth in his neck. A strip of flesh torn way.

Kai flops on the floor like a landed fish creating its own pool to swim in, the wound pumping bright red.

The doors open. Sean stares at Ali crouched over Kai's body, at Kai going still. Sean remembers the way the wolf looked at him up on the hill.

He runs. Runs like he wishes Ali could have run. Runs flat-out, head down. Runs with all his heart. Out across the platform, up the stairs, hurdling the turnstile, onto the street, vaguely aware that Jazz is there with him, that he is not alone in his horror and fear, companionship counting for less than nothing in this moment.

⊙

They run out of steam near a stand of rental bikes, are left bent over, sucking air, praying that they've put enough distance between them and . . . and . . .

"What?" Jazz says between inhalations. "What the . . . ? What? What?"

Sean doesn't know.

Except he knows.

"Something . . ." He pants. "Something with the mind-jack. When . . . the wolf . . ." He can't finish the thought.

"What?" Jazz is crying. "Kai." That's all she says. Just his name. An entire world of hurt in a word. A whole truncated life.

They go back to the mindjack place. Can't think what else to do. They're too scared to head back down to the subway so they take the rental bikes across the Williamsburg Bridge. Manhattan glitters at them, its lights suddenly become malevolent: yellow eyes peering out of the forest.

The store is thrumming with activity. A queue out the door. People yell as they barge past. The guy at the desk looks up, pissed. Not even half as pissed as Sean. Not even half as afraid even when Sean grabs him by the lapels and hauls him half across the counter and screams in his face for answers.

People drag Sean off the guy, but Sean doesn't stop yelling.

"I don't know, man." The counter-guy sweaty with fear.

"I just work here. I don't write the damn code. It's Omni you want. They make the stuff."

Sean finds the address for the Omni headquarters online, rents a car from a 24-hour place in an underground parking lot, makes the drive out onto Long Island with Jazz nearly catatonic in the seat next to him. Eventually she falls asleep.

He sits in the car in the parking lot outside Omni HQ, waits for dawn to arrive.

He slides down in his seat when the security guard comes to unlock the place. Jazz is still out cold in the passenger seat. He watches the guard go in through the double doors, disappear off somewhere. He sprints across the parking lot and through the front doors. A satisfied sigh is coming from a restroom. A keycard rests upon the front desk. Sean grabs it, make a dash for a stairwell, heads upward, taking the stairs two at a time.

He's waiting when the executive enters her office, ambushes her while she's still holding her Starbucks. He's wielding a stapler and a heavy glass paperweight.

"My girlfriend." He's slurring with shock and sleep-deprivation. "She was 'jacked into a sheep, killed by a wolf. And afterward…" He's shaking so hard as he tells her about Kai and the train that he drops the stapler. She helps into a desk chair, has him walk her through it one more time.

"Sort some of feedback error," she says. "They're incredibly rare. We cover it in the terms and agreements, though."

Sean explains how little he cares about terms and agreements in blunt but colorful terms.

The woman shrugs. "You both signed a waiver."

Sean screams, "Where is my girlfriend?"

Security guards arrive very shortly after that. But the executive waves them down. "Well," she says, "I don't know for sure, but, if I had to start somewhere, I'd try to find the wolf whose mindjacked your girlfriend."

Sean stares at her. "Find . . . ?"

She shrugs. "You both signed a waiver."

He lunges at her, and this time she doesn't wave security off. They drag him downstairs, dump him outside, and tell him they're going to call the cops.

He walks back to the car, still fuming. He stops when he sees the smear of red across the windshield.

Jazz is hanging half out of the passenger door. Something has smashed the glass, must have dragged her out. He can see the scratch marks clawed into her skin, the ragged bite wounds, the missing chunks of flesh swallowed by a hungry gullet.

He looks around. How did nobody see this? What did this?

Except he knows exactly what did.

The wolf is hunting them.

☉

The guy in the mindjack place quails behind his counter. "I told you, man . . ."

"The sheep," Sean not screaming anymore, voice now held as steady as knife to a man's throat. "Where are the sheep we 'jack?"

The drive upstate takes two days. He has to crash in a motel after the first few hours on the road, unable to keep his eyes open any longer. In the room, he dreams of running across an open field, something chasing him, and all around him sheep bleating so loud it sounds like they're screaming. He wakes in a cold sweat, looks out the window at the car parked below. There's only one other car parked in the lot. He shivers.

He hits the road early, trying to rationalize away his fears. If a wolf really has mindjacked Ali, how can it pursue him? A wolf can't drive.

Except it found them out on Long Island.

Sean eases his foot down on the accelerator.

He parks the car in Lake Placid and asks around about the local farms. A woman with a kind face sells him an old map and makes circles on it for him. He heads out into the hills.

The first farm is a bust. At the second, the farmer treats him like a pervert, threatens him with a shotgun. Danny approaches the third with more circumspection, avoids the farmhouse and heads directly to the fields.

He recognizes it almost immediately: the slope of the hill, the feel of the grass beneath his feet, the smell in the air. He's been here before. He sets off up the slope, scanning desperately for the flock, straddling fences and forging small streams. Above him, clouds swirl across the sky, pooling, casting the day in shades of gray.

Below him, he sees a car pull up outside the farmhouse, a small dark figure climbs out, her hair blowing in the wind.

He knows there's no way he can tell if it's Ali or not from this distance.

He can tell.

Sean redoubles his pace, ascends at an unsustainable half-run. Ten minutes later, he finds himself leaning against a fence post gasping. He looks back.

The figure is crossing the fields behind him.

He goes on up, praying that every crest will reveal the flock. He looks back.

She's closing the gap.

Around a bend, up, through a small concavity between two shallow rises of earth, he discovers a small protected bowl of earth. And there they are. God, he recognizes some of them. He sees the familiar cant of an ovine eye, the stubbiness of an ear, the squareness of a nose. He has stood among these sheep, been one of them.

"Ali?" he has to ask, has to call her name. In case he made a mistake. In case the feedback loop worked differently from how the executive explained it. In case she's here. Please, God, let her be here.

The sheep ignore him. The hillside ignores him. The wind and the sky ignore him.

He is standing still, and the wolf is getting closer.

There are woods to the north. He remembers the beast standing with them as a backdrop, brazen in its bloodlust.

He heads uphill, toward the nearest tangle of trees, pushes in. He thinks how much easier this would be mindjacked into a red-tailed hawk or a fox, except he's never 'jacking in to anything again. Not ever. So he's left like this, in this body, unable to track scent or subtle trails, just blundering about terrified and desperate.

"Ali!" he calls. "Ali!"

She doesn't respond. Can't, he supposes. He keeps calling anyway.

"Ali!"

And then, on the air, a long, wailing howl.

An answer.

He breaks into a run. Branches scratch and scrape at him. Leaves and brambles mire him. But he runs on because he's not running away anymore. He's running *toward*. Toward her.

"Ali!"

The growl stops him. A single bass note. He turns around.

It's Ali's body. She still has the face that blinked sleepily at him across the pillows every day when the alarm went off. Still has the hands that eased the tension from his shoulders when work was driving him utterly insane. Still has the stomach that once rumbled so loudly after Taco Tuesday that it woke him up from a dead sleep.

But those are not Ali's eyes. Those are not her thoughts that pull her lips back from her teeth.

Ali's body glides through the trees toward him, stops just ten yards away, snarling. He's frozen, trying to work out what she's doing, what will come next, why she isn't just ending it.

Then he sees them slinking through the trees, emerging all around: wolves in every shade of brown, and gray, and black. Thick furred and shaggy. Fangs forward. Hackles up. Wolves on every side of him.

Ali's body—the wolf inside it—smiles.

Except then something presses against Sean's leg. A hot, heavy presence. And he looks down, and maybe it is because he has seen her in so many skins before, or maybe it is because the way she moves is ever-so slightly different from every other animal there, or maybe it's because their hearts are entangled at a quantum level—he doesn't know, but he *knows* that it's Ali.

It feels like the whole world is growling. The sound thrumming through the real Ali and into his leg and radiating out into every wolf there. And Ali's body—the wolf inside it—lets out a sound like a roar. And real Ali barks back. And all the wolves start to close in on Sean's pursuer. Like jaws upon a throat.

He closes his eyes as the wolves reach Ali's body. As they drown it in their snarling, biting, clawing fury. He closes his eyes, and sinks to his knees, and holds on to Ali, to the wolf she has become, to the press of her warm flank, and the wetness of nose, and the muscles in her flanks, and to all that he has left, as her body is torn apart.

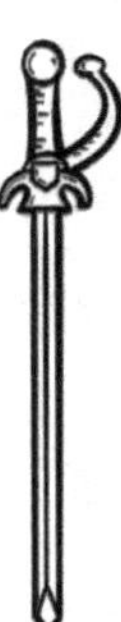

In Time With the Ocean

~ *Devan Barlow*

"You don't know how relieved I am that you're in town," Cassie said softly.

Now that they'd been sitting across from one another in the coffee shop for a few minutes, Val could see the other woman looked almost unchanged since the last time they'd seen each other, though Cassie's manner was so different it was hard to tell. Val had never seen her this unsettled.

Then again, Val wanted to believe she too was very different. She had only come back into town for her grandmother's funeral, which had been the day before. The last thing she'd expected this morning was for Cassie to show up at the house, hoping Val's parents could share her phone number and instead finding Val herself.

Cassie let out a breath, then said, "The five of us got together last night."

Of course they were all still friends. Val felt an invisible pull, drawing her back into patterns she had never really chosen to be a part of.

"Last night," Cassie continued, "you know, for the anniversary?"

Val nodded, warily. They had all graduated high school ten years ago.

"I mean we get together a lot, but this time . . . Jo ordered us all to bring the water bottles from that night." Cassie's worry was momentary replaced by wryness, as she acknowledged that particular dynamic hadn't changed with time. "So we could toast with them."

"Please tell me you didn't actually *drink* that stuff?" Val asked.

"I thought it would be vile," Cassie said hurriedly. "So I only took a little sip . . . except it was," she lowered her voice, "really *good*."

"How many drinks in were you by this point?"

"This was my first!" Cassie protested. "Ok, I think Gavin had started before we got there, but I hadn't, and everyone else thought it was tasty too. So we just kept drinking it —"

"So good to see the two of you together!" gushed a passing woman as she headed out the door with a to-go cup. Cassie flashed her a bright, brittle smile, which had dissolved by the time Val realized this was their high school's librarian. Val couldn't help feeling vaguely insulted by the assumption she was the same person she had been a decade before. She wasn't sure that was rational, and she wasn't sure what it said about her that it bothered her so much.

"By the time I finished the bottle," Cassie said, "I was hearing . . . something. Like waves, but not? No one else seemed to, until . . ." she leaned forward over the table, knocking over her cup, and Val's hands shot out to keep it from spilling hot coffee over both of them. "Jo started saying weird things, at first I thought she was drunk, but they weren't . . . I don't know how she made those sounds. Then she attacked Gavin."

"What?!"

By now Cassie's words were barely audible. "She jumped on top of him, pinned him to the couch, and then she . . . *she bit his neck.* There was blood everywhere, we were all screaming but she wouldn't stop."

Val stared, forgetting the small horrors of her return in light of what she was hearing.

Which was when she noticed Cassie's eyes, and how the liquid inside them seemed to be spinning.

"Sonia was still sober enough to call an ambulance, but . . . the paramedics couldn't get Jo off Gavin, finally they sedated her but he'd lost so much blood, we were at the hospital all night but they're not sure if either of them will make it and I keep *hearing* the *ocean*!"

After another few, stunned moments, Val finally said, "this is horrifying. But what do you want me—"

"You were there that night!" Cassie's hands shook. "Oh God, please tell me you still have it? Your water bottle?"

"My—"

"The ocean wants them back. That's why it won't leave me alone. Before I left the hospital this morning, to go to your parents', Patrick said he heard it too. The ocean knows we took its water that night and it wants it *back*!"

Her voice spiked high and loud, turning heads in their direction.

Cassie gestured her outside, away from the scrutiny, and tried another tactic. "It's like that time we needed a sixth person for the French presentation, you remember? You're our missing piece!"

Frustration finally overpowered Val's confusion. "Your *missing piece*?" she snapped. "Am I the only one who remembers how that night ended?!"

On the way to the cove, Val was scrunched uncomfortably, sharing the middle back seat with Cassie. Sonia, taciturn as usual, stared out the window on their left, as Patrick on their right enthused about the coming summer. Gavin drove, and of course Jo was perched in the front seat, making the occasional barbed comment about people from school. The air was fresh and bright, as full of possibility as it was of sea salt, and their last batch of high school finals was over.

Val wasn't really part of this group, except for French class. Neither their high school nor the school's French enrollment was large, so they had all been in the class together since sixth grade, and been each other's conversational partners more times than she could count. Val had somehow become their chosen sixth whenever an even number was needed, but Jo and her followers were a sacred, much-envied quintet at their school. Val had never been invited to join them for something that wasn't class-related, but, surprising even herself somewhat, she had said yes when Jo invited her to the cove with them today.

They hopped the barriers around the cove. No one was supposed to swim here, after the rash of accidents the previous summer, but the six of them were the only ones around. Besides, none of the adults in town had ever seemed immune to Jo's charm, or her parents' money.

Val's stomach rumbled. The beach always made her hungry.

Gavin produced junk food from his car. Cassie grinned and ripped open a bag of chips, only for Jo to sneer and say "greedy much?" Sonia giggled nastily. Val frowned and reached for some chips of her own, as Cassie gave her a quick look of thanks.

As they spread out beach towels, Gavin also handed out plastic water bottles. Val took one, only to choke when her first sip revealed it was filled with not water, but vodka. Jo rolled her eyes, then took a practiced drink from her own bottle.

Val only pretended to sip after that, and poured splashes of vodka onto the sand when no one was looking. She didn't like the taste, and figured at least one of them should be in some kind of state to make sure everyone got home. She thought, though, that maybe she liked being with them.

Or at least she liked being with Patrick and Cassie. Patrick was the one she knew the best, since they had the most other classes together, and he'd been the one to ask her to join their group for the year's final French project, a presentation about Molière including a staged scene from *Tartuffe*. And Cassie was friendlier than all the rest of them put together, especially if you were willing to listen to her retell urban legends about all the people who had drowned at this cove over the years.

Val wasn't sure why these two let Jo order them around, but had long since given up trying to understand this group. Jo provided a wildly confident drumbeat the other four marched unthinkingly along to, despite the fact she never seemed to be nice, not even to her friends.

As the night darkened, a warm softness settled over them. Val wasn't entirely sure what they had all been talking about, but at some point she realized she was leaning her head on Patrick's shoulder, and Cassie was on her other side, drowsily braiding her hair.

Suddenly, Gavin lurched up from the sand and started grabbing everyone's water bottles. "We can't forget this night!" he declared. They laughed at him as he stumbled around in the surf and filled each bottle with seawater. "To remember our triumph!" He screwed the caps back on and returned them. "Keep them safe!"

Val nodded and tucked her bottle into the tote bag she'd brought with her, though privately she wondered how much of this night Gavin would actually remember.

As Gavin flopped back down on the sand, Jo stretched as if she was trying to wake herself up, looked at Val, and said, "Oh. You're still here?"

Val went cold. Patrick gave Jo a look, but Jo only tossed her hair, though several long blonde strands caught in her lip gloss. "I didn't realize you were standing *right there* when I mentioned coming here, but you're so, like, pathetic, and Madame was nearby and you know she hasn't given us our grade for the project yet so . . ." she leaned back as if there was any remaining tan to be gleaned from the light of the moon, serene despite the hair still lodged in pink gloss. "I didn't think you'd actually *come.*"

Val was particularly glad she hadn't had more than that first sip of vodka, because it meant she had no trouble storming off the beach and getting herself home.

It was the last time she had spoken to any of them.

"*Please,*" Cassie implored as she followed Val down the street outside the coffee shop. "Please, at least look for it, meet me at the cove tonight . . . you don't understand, with Jo, we've known her forever and she's always had us, well, enthralled . . ."

Val sped up, unwilling to listen to any more. By the time she finished the short walk back to her parents' house, she was prepared to grit her teeth, take the familial guilt, and get herself on the next flight home. Until she found her parents in the living room, watching local news.

". . . both victims of the bizarre accident died this morning, while two more were brought in several hours later. One died almost immediately, while the other is still in critical condition . . ."

"Val, honey," her dad said, shuddering as he turned away from the television, "hope you had a nice time with your friend?"

Back in her old room, Val dug through the closet until finally, within a box within a larger box, under a hat she didn't remember owning and several random cables for electronics she was pretty sure her parents no longer had, she found the tote bag she'd brought to the cove that night, with the water bottle wrapped inside.

The label had long since ripped away, but the cap remained firmly on, protecting the scummy seawater and leftover vodka sloshing inside.

Aggravation with Cassie and her friends and this whole *place* propelled her to the bathroom sink to pour the liquid down the drain.

Until she heard it. Fast, and rippling outward as though it began deep inside her own bones—no, not that close, as if it started inside the *bottle*.

The world softened and blurred. Memory-that-wasn't-memory seized her. She was encompassed by the sense of ocean, deeper than she could ever dream to swim herself, and the awareness of creatures who fed on blood. Who sometimes had to push further upward through the ocean than they preferred, who were at risk from engines, equipment—her limbs thrashed as the creature was caught, mangled, its blood going every which way through the water until some few drops of it finally reached the shore—where some unlikely alchemy of seawater and time and the night's emotions and the slick of vodka clinging to the inside of the bottle . . . preserved the *blood*—

The sensation of slimy liquid making its way down her throat snapped her back to reality. The bottle was open and pressed to her lips. She gagged, but it was too late.

It was impossible to distinguish between the vile taste of the water, and the sharp tang of fear coating her mouth.

The whole way to the cove, Val's mind whirled. She had wanted Jo and her followers to like her, much as she was ashamed to admit it. She was nearly certain she no longer care about them liking her, but she didn't want them *dead*.

Except three of them already were. But could this ridiculous idea of Cassie's, appeasing the ocean, save the rest? Val didn't know, but she couldn't outpace that *sound*, and the memories-that-weren't.

She heard Cassie a moment before she saw her. A strange noise, both sinuous and sharp, as if the ocean's roar had been condensed and twisted until it was something that could come out of a human mouth. Cassie's movement had altered since that morning. Now she walked like something sloshed underneath her skin, an agitated liquid that kept her swaying from side to side as it tried to escape.

"It's so angry," Cassie said, and Val saw her teeth had become pointed. "It's so hungry . . ." Cassie's familiar brown eyes, still rippling, were now fixated on Val's neck.

"Ow!" Cassie had stepped out of her strappy sandals as she approached, and now cradled one bare foot in her hand. A small droplet of red pushed up from a new split in the skin.

As Val saw the blood, the sound that had been haunting her intensified, roaring up from both the ocean and a place between her ribs, in furious waves that echoed in her blood. A luminous song of blood and ocean depths, insisting that she was out of place, insisting that she must feed so she had the strength to return to the deep, to her true home where she could *thrive*. Insisting there was no feast more nourishing than another whose blood pulsed in time with the ocean.

She opened the bottle.

Desperate, hungry hope shone in Cassie's eyes.

Val sipped. It was disgusting—

It was—

Perfect.

And the beach always made her hungry.

IV

The Alphabet of Dread

~ Ben Curl

. . . you've seen what troubles I endured to reconstruct this lost code. There's no reason you should still be reading this. There's no reason for me to keep writing it. No reason except . . . once you trace one of the characters with your hand, or even with your mind, you can't stop. You can't stop tracing their patterns, plumbing their meanings, until the series is complete. The letters have a logic of their own. It's a rhythmic sequence that transcends all understanding.

Whatever the preceding pages were, they'd been ripped from the yellowed chapbook. Cal and I were leaning over the bar, reading in silence, in the red haze that defines my memory of Brut's Local History Museum and Pub. I don't remember the faces of the regulars we met that night. I can't recall their names. When I think of that night, the thing that comes back is the haze.

The regulars were nice, friendly folk, exactly the kind you'd imagine stumbling across in the northern Midwest on a night like that, when we stopped driving because the snow off Lake Superior was wiping the road clean out of sight. Cal was right to have us pull off and search for a motel, though I said he was being ridiculous. After we'd checked in, we couldn't bear staying in our room, listening to the wind, just the two of us, staring at a rabbit-eared TV that didn't work. We'd had enough of our partnered solitude during our time in the Porcupine Mountains. Neither of us said it, but we needed a break. A break from each other.

At least, that's what I was needing. With Cal, it was always hard to tell. He'd never tell me directly when he was getting sick of me. I had to make educated guesses. On this particular night, I made my guess when he put on his headphones (which I knew (and he knew that I knew) no longer worked).

The chapbook had no words on its cover. There was only an ink drawing. I don't know if you could even call it a drawing. It was the impression of the beginning of a drawing. It didn't bring any animal, object, or idea to mind. If it was a symbol, it was unlike any we'd ever seen. I'm trying not to remember it, now that I know what happens if you look too long at those lines, but it was something like an "S" intersected by a "C" with horns and hooks on the ends of the curves.

(It's best if you forget what I said it looked like. When you think of it, or any other symbol I mention, summon a blank space on a page in your mind.)

Cal was going to push the chapbook aside to look at the diorama it was sitting on. The rectangular glass box of figurines, one of many in the bar, showed the town of Ontonagon in the 1870s. Other boxes held the town in other phases of its existence: as a mining town, a logging town, a receding town ("The end of the world," the man two stools down called it).

I picked up the chapbook, not feeling all that interested, but with nothing else to do, still looking for the encounter that would distract me from whatever was going on between Cal and me.

"*The Alphabet of Dread, reconstructed and annotated by Dr. Vassago,*" I read aloud, and flipped the page to be greeted by a splintering fork of ink.

When I was a child, staying at my great-aunt's house, sleeping in a narrow attic, something rattled behind the closet door. It sounded like one of those rain sticks you make when you're in elementary school, with the paper towel tube filled with rice. No rodent could have made that rattling. I pulled the quilt over my head. I didn't pull it back until morning, until my great-aunt called me down for breakfast. I ran down the steep stairs so fast I almost fell.

I hadn't remembered that sound, that sleepless night, until the moment I saw that character in the chapbook.

The image, bereft of any obvious meaning, evoked the rattle I'd suppressed for all those years.

I glanced at Cal. He was hard to read as ever. Silent as stone. Inscrutable as a splatter of ink.

           ☉

This one draws forth the hidden meaning of closed doors.

If you inscribe it on any part of your home that is made of wood or stone, then all the doors in your house will slam shut.

All, except for one.

Do not go through that door. Shut it! Shut it fast!

"Where are you two staying?" the woman with short red hair asked. (I remember her hair. I remember she owned the local paper. I remember the way she shook Cal's hand. What I don't remember is her face, her name, anything else that would help me recognize her if we ever met again.)

Cal told her the name of the place. She commented on the owner, how he was probably going to retire soon. Cal asked polite questions. Their conversation faded.

I was lost in a torrent of whispers coming from outside the bar, from some place I shouldn't have been able to hear.

This one was passed around Antwerp in crisp, square, yellow envelopes. It proliferated in the days leading up to the city's fall to the Spanish in 1576, again before the Siege of 1832. No one has identified the illustrators, though several copies remain intact in the archives of the Plantin-Moretus Museum.

They stopped exhibiting the copies after a string of violent confrontations broke out among visitors in the gallery. They moved them to the archives.

They stopped keeping the copies in an unlocked drawer when the employees assigned to that part of the archive kept bashing their skulls to pieces against the metal filing cabinets.

Cal was sipping a beer. The bartender had given us each a round, plastic token ("for the next time you're in town") but we knew that wasn't likely to happen. Without either of us saying it, we both knew there was a good chance this would be our last trip together. We'd ruined the Upper Peninsula for each other, it seemed.

"Why are you still reading that thing?" His low voice was drenched with disdain. "Socialize. Stop being a creep."

"You're always so concerned about what people will think of me." I didn't lift my eyes from the pages. "You're embarrassed by me."

"No, that's not it."

"Then what is it?"

"Maybe we just need some time apart."

There, he had finally said it.

Fucking coward.

Whenever my former colleague, Professor Gamigin, spoke of this one, she held her sleeve over her mouth. Her muffled words were unintelligible. She said you had to talk about it, to get it off your chest, but it was important that no one ever heard what you said. Across the lowlands I gathered many reports of this character being found scratched into the planks of shipwrecks hauled from the North Sea.

One evening, while walking back from her studio apartment, I asked Professor Gamigin about it yet again, determined to find out what she was hiding from me. She put her velvet glove over her lips and pointed to a patch of sky between a bank turret and a church spire, where a tiny black cloud was unraveling, growing larger by the second.

Then she slapped me across my mouth and that was the end of us. All exchanges between us from then on were curt and professional, nothing more.

"Hey, seriously, put that thing down. You look spooked."

Cal's eyes burned light blue when he was affectionate, cobalt blue when he was angry, and a swirling mixture when he was afraid. While he stared at me, I couldn't make out the color of his eyes. The red haze had seeped into everything.

"Are you hearing things too?" I asked. "Are you remembering strange feelings?"

He put an elbow on the bar, nested the back of his head in his palm, and studied me from an awkward angle. This was something he only did when he was afraid. Specifically, he did it when he was afraid of something he had to say.

"Gary, yes, I'm hearing things too."

I didn't expect this. I thought he would take some kind of optimistic, get-your-head-out-of-the-darkness approach. That was his go-to. He always tried to spin my negative thoughts aside. He was always trying to fix me. He honestly surprised me when he said, "I'm feeling things I thought were buried away in my nightmares—my most private nightmares—the ones I never remember during the day. That's why I'm asking you to stop reading it."

Something inside me broke. It was a good break. A clean break. Like a bone.

"Why aren't you trying to fix me?"

"What?"

"You're not trying to deny my feelings. I just—" I twiddled the pamphlet in my fingers, rustling the pages. I lost track of whatever I was about to say. A stark line intersected by three sharp barbs distracted me.

Everything began to spin.

The moose head above the bar, with its glassy eyes, made me want to cry. Those eyes were so gentle. How could such gentleness be in such a gigantic head?

When gentle things die, where do they go?

"I don't want us to end like this." I spoke to an empty, spinning pub. When I say empty, I mean there were no human occupants, but there were others. There were the taxidermied animals in the display boxes along the ceiling: a pair of prancing foxes, a wild-eyed rabbit, a sleek bobcat, a grouse. There was the wooden sculpture of a Jesuit missionary in snowshoes, the Ojibwa woman in her dress, a porcelain Elvis.

I couldn't see anyone else but I could hear the voices: the bartender, the man two stools down from us, Cal.

" . . . a seizure?"

"It'd be quicker to drive him then to wait for an ambulance."

"We can't drive in this."

"Don't move him. It's too dangerous."

"Gary, hold on, just hold on . . ."

That was the end.

I never came back. Without words, without sight, without any conscious link with my surroundings, my brain stopped in the ICU of the smallest hospital still operating in the country. I watched it all happen from outside the hospital window, thirty feet above, looking down on Cal beside me, his hand on top of my hand. The snow drifted between my disembodied presence and the window.

The snow made curving figures, fleeting things that never materialized.

I never managed to tell him how much I appreciated his vulnerability in that moment at Brut's Local History Museum and Pub, how I felt more connected with him than ever when he admitted that he was scared too.

Why couldn't he have said something like this before? Why did it take that damned chapbook? And now it was too damned late.

⊙

Don't try to picture the symbols. Forget I ever said anything.

Blank pages.

Make blank pages in your mind wherever you think of that book.

This one is the final letter. Look at the way the hooks become feet. The hash marks turn into the first stirrings of what will someday become human hands.

Yes, this is what I've come to believe, after many years of studying this ancient alphabet. These shapes are vague outlines of what we will, or may, become.

The patterns precede language. Before we were human, we sensed these shapes. When we were single-celled organisms, these intersections of lines made us feel whatever an individual cell can feel. They lured us. They lure us still. It's at the cellular level these shapes work on us. That's why it's no use trying to outthink them.

There's only one way past. You must outrun them.

You must forget them.

That's the secret of human bravery, the greatest triumph of the human mind: the power to forget.

Sometimes these characters give you flashes of what may be. Then, in an instant, you return to where you were. In that moment, don't hesitate. Don't do what I've done. Don't live in the frozen dance of the Alphabet of Dread.

Sincerely, Dr. Vassago.

⊙

"Hey, seriously, put that thing down. You look spooked."

Cal's blue eyes pierced the red haze, hauling me back into the world that was only him and me. He leaned in. He put his hand on my knee.

"Are you hearing things too?" I asked. "Are you remembering strange feelings?"

"Yeah, I'm hearing things too. I'm feeling things I thought were buried away in my nightmares—my most private nightmares—the ones I never remember during the day. That's why I'm asking you to stop reading it."

I didn't hesitate—not this time. I shoved the pamphlet over the edge of the bar, to the bartender's feet. I put my hand on his elbow. I kissed him on the cheek. I wouldn't let this be our last trip.

"I love you, Cal."

"I love you too, Gary."

"Great. Then let's get the hell out of here."

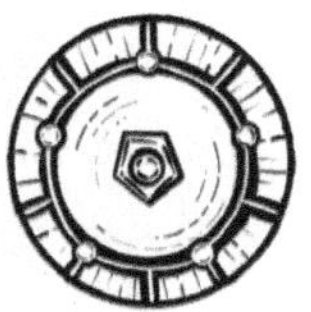

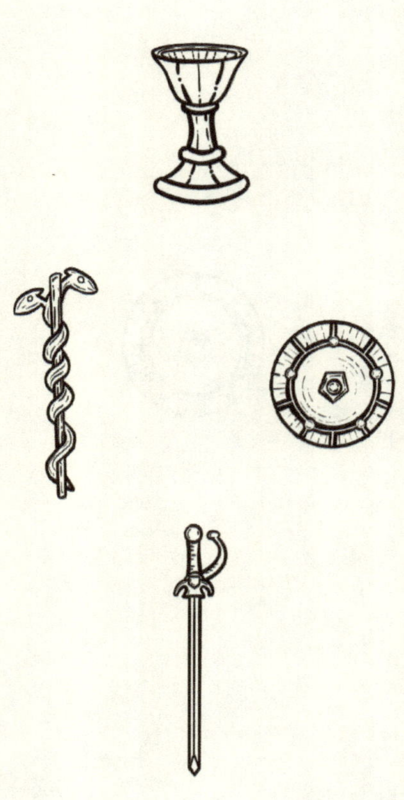

CONTRIBUTORS

Pen Anderson

Pen Anderson has spent the past two and a half decades in an assorted series of disciplines from summer camp counselor to Internet publisher, graphic designer, illustrator, software engineer, sound designer, audio/video installation artist, courier, miniaturist, and tabletop game facilitator. He lives in Chicago with his wife, cats, and their (fully grown) children, where together they have recently founded a family business, Pentacle Games.

This collection debuts his first published fiction, but you can find mixed-media broadcasts, photography, epiphanies, and ephemera on Bluesky at bsky.app/profile/pensiv.art

Devan Barlow

Devan Barlow is the author of the *Curses & Curtains* series of fairy tales-meet-musicals fantasy novels, and the collection *Foolish Hopes and Spilled Entrails: Retellings*. Her short fiction and poetry have appeared in various anthologies and magazine. She reads voraciously, and can often be found hanging out with her dog, drinking tea, and thinking about sea monsters. devanbarlow.com, Bluesky: @devanbarlow.bsky.social

Megan Lee Beals

Megan Lee Beals writes cozy and fanciful horrors from her home in the perpetually soggy Pacific Northwest. She lives with her husband, her twin son and daughter, and the family's formally feral cat. When she isn't writing or chasing toddlers, Megan is drawing or sewing or building, and generally trying to accumulate hobbies at a truly unsustainable rate. She has been published in *Translunar Traveler's Lounge* and *The Iowa Review*. You can find more of her various things at www.meganleebeals.com.

Elou Carroll

Elou Carroll writes spooky, whimsical, and strange stories. Her work appears or is forthcoming in *The Deadlands, Baffling Magazine, FOUND #2, Flash Fiction Online, Cosmic Horror Monthly* and others. When she's not hoarding skeleton keys and whispering with ghosts, she can be found editing *Crow & Cross Keys*, publishing all things dark and lovely, and loitering on instagram (@keychilde) and bsky (@keychild.bsky.social). She keeps a catalogue of her weird little wordcreatures on www.eloucarroll.com.

Ben Curl

Ben Curl is an author, playwright, and performer. His short stories appear in numerous indie publications. His performances materialize in bookshops, community centers, theaters, and alleys. He also conducts creative workshops and hosts the Capital Letters Eclectic Fiction Club at A Novel Concept bookshop in Lansing, MI, where he resides with his son, a dog, a tarantula, and a menagerie of clay puppets.

Jetse de Vries

Jetse de Vries has travelled all five continents. He nearly froze to death at Salar de Uyuni, suffered heatstroke in Purnululu, got lost in Ahmednagar, faced elephants in Maamba, and has witnessed ten total solar eclipses.

He's had over sixty short stories published, was part of the *Interzone* editorial team and edited *Shine*—an anthology of optimistic SF for Solaris Books. Check out his substack *The Divergent Panorama*: https://jetse.substack.com.

Daniel David Froid

Daniel David Froid is the author of *My Home Is Not There*, a chapbook published by Bottlecap Press. His stories appear in *Lightspeed, Nightmare, Black Warrior Review, Post Road*, and elsewhere. He lives in Arizona.

H. L. Fullerton

H. L. Fullerton writes short fiction—mostly speculative, occasionally about dead things—which can be found in more than 50 anthologies and magazines including *Kaleidotrope, Tales of Terror* and *Underland Arcana* (issues 2, 8, and 10). You may find them on Bluesky as @HLFullerton.bsky.social.

Brian U. Garrison

Brian U. Garrison (he/him) writes poetry for children, adults, and grand adults. His chapbook *Micropoetry for Microplanets* (Space Cowboy Books) celebrates the smallish to medium rocks that circle our sun. The book also provides a fun excuse to talk to students about space (and what a lovely, inhabitable planet we have here on Earth).

He currently serves as President of the Science Fiction & Fantasy Poetry Association and Managing Editor for *Eye to the Telescope* (eyetothetelescope.com). Find him online at bugthewriter.com or enjoying the vegan biscuits and gravy at Shoofly Cafe in Portland, Oregon.

Basile Lebret

Basile Lebret is French and lives south of Paris. After a career in the movie industry, he's come back to writing short stories, comic books and screenplays. His work has been published in SlicedUp Press' *Monstroddities*, Atonic Vision's *Strange Weeds*, Bag of Bones' *Step Into the Light*, Off Topic Publishing's *Home*, Underland Press' *Even Cozier Cosmic*, Dark Moon Rising's *The Devil's Playground*, *The Best of Carnage House Year One* and the Lufthunger Club's *Les Feux de la Révolte*. Find him on any network: @evoripclaw.

Jonathan Wood

Jonathan Wood is an Englishman in New York, albeit the state and not the city. He has previously published seven comedic fantasy novels and one fantasy novel that is only a little bit funny. He enjoys writing flash fiction, which can be found at jonathanwood.substack.com.

PAMELA COLMAN SMITH

The tarot images in this issue of Arcana are from the deck illustrated by Pamela Colman Smith. It was released in 1909 as the Rider-Waite deck (so named, at that time, in reference to its publisher, William Rider & Son). It remains the most influential and widely used tarot deck. While the impetus for the deck came from Arthur Edward Waite, Colman Smith was responsible for the iconography of the cards.

Pamela Colman Smith also illustrated over twenty books, wrote two collections of Jamaican folklore, edited two magazines, and ran the Green Sheaf Press, a small press devoted to women writers. She continued to write and illustrate throughout her life.

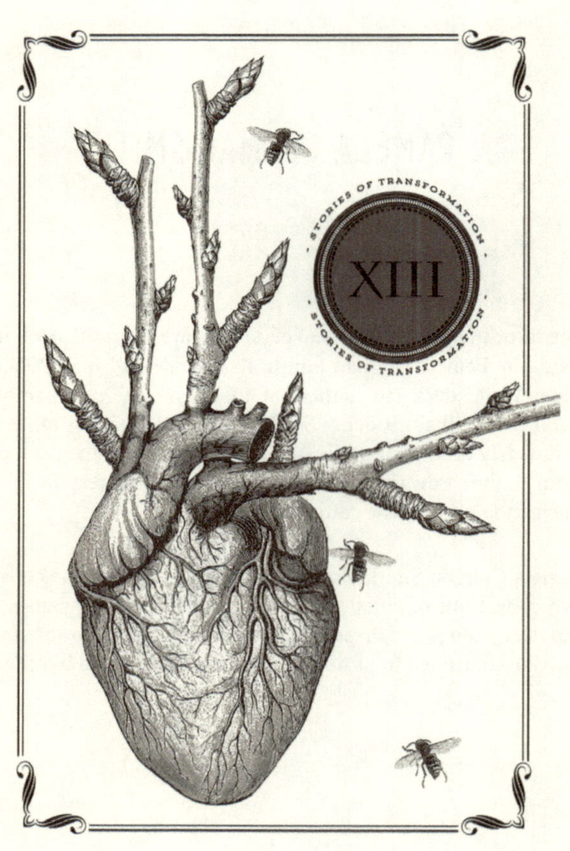

STORIES OF TRANSFORMATION
XIII
STORIES OF TRANSFORMATION

XIII

The thirteenth Tarot card is Death, and he is a symbol not of the end, but of transformation and rebirth. This is the genesis and root of *Thirteen: Stories of Transformation*. The twenty-eight authors of this collection are voices—new and old—who are not afraid to explore what comes next. Whether it be a life after death, a life without love, a life filled with hunger, or the life shared by a ghost. These are stories of the weird, the mythic, the fantastic, the futuristic, the supernatural, and the horrific.

With stories by Liz Argall • M. David Blake • Richard Bowes • George Cotronis • Amanda C. Davis • Julie C. Day • Jetse de Vries • Jennifer Giesbrecht • Daryl Gregory • Rik Hoskin • Rebecca Kuder • Claude Lalumière • Marc Levinthal • Grá Linnaea • Alex Dally MacFarlane • Juli Mallett • Lyn McConchie • Fiona Moore • Gregory L. Norris • Adrienne J. Odasso • Cat Rambo • Andrew Penn Romine • David Tallerman • Tais Teng Richard Thomas • Fran Wilde • A. C. Wise • Christie Yant

Edited by Mark Teppo.

Available at independent bookstores everywhere.

http://www.underlandpress.com

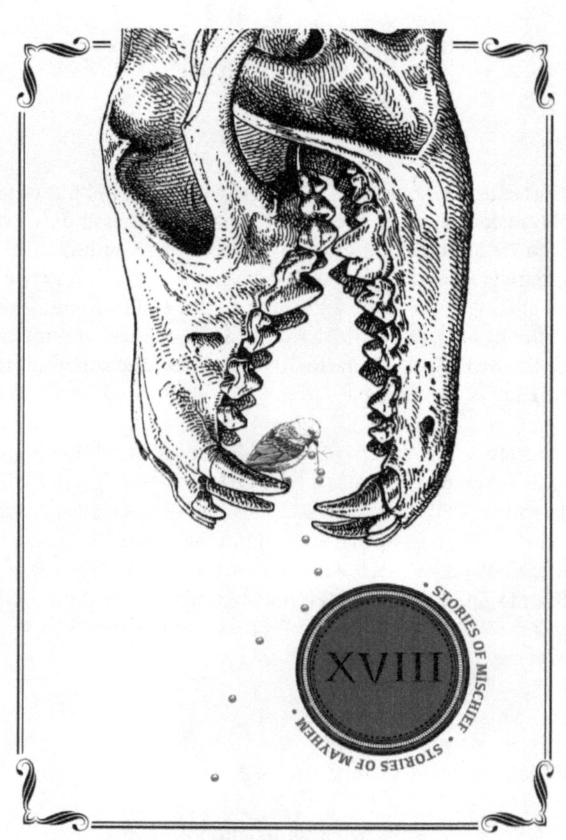
XVIII
STORIES OF MISCHIEF
STORIES OF MAYHEM

XVIII

The eighteenth Tarot card is the Moon, and those who raise their arms to her know she offers Mercy and Severity in equal measure. This is the great river at night, where wolves howl and all doors are open. All futures are possible, and every truth is elusive. This is the source and passion of *Eighteen: Stories of Mischief & Mayhem*. These twenty-four stories from voices—old and new—celebrate the inevitability of fate, the horror of prophecy, and the shivering delight of not knowing what comes next.

Cross over the threshold with us, and explore the strange, the weird, and the fantastic. Do not fear what lies ahead. It is the same as what came before. The only difference is you. This is *Eighteen*, and nothing will be the same.

With stories by Forrest Aguirre • Darin Bradley • Christopher East • Scott Edelman • Nicole Feldringer • Ben Gamblin • Ingrid Garcia • A. P. Howell • Emma Johnson-Rivard • E. E. King • Jessie Kwak • Shannon Lawrence • Gerri Leen • Mark Mills • Christi Nogle Tammie Painter • Josh Rountree • Erica Sage • Lorraine Schein • J. Dee Stanley • Richard Thomas • John Waterfall • Wendy N. Wagner • Todd Zack

Edited by Mark Teppo.

Available at independent bookstores everywhere.

http://www.underlandpress.com

* 9 7 8 1 6 3 0 2 3 1 2 8 6 *